Pauline Bradford Hopkins

Mademoiselle de Berny

A Story of Valley Forge

Pauline Bradford Hopkins

Mademoiselle de Berny
A Story of Valley Forge

ISBN/EAN: 9783744747615

Printed in Europe, USA, Canada, Australia, Japan

Cover: Foto ©Andreas Hilbeck / pixelio.de

More available books at **www.hansebooks.com**

Mademoiselle de Berny

Armand at Heyward's quarters
Valley Forge.

page 98

Mademoiselle de Berny

A Story of Valley Forge

By
Pauline Bradford Mackie

Illustrated by
Frank T. Merrill

" In their ragged regimentals
Stood the old Continentals,
Yielding not "

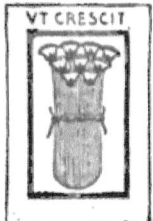

VT CRESCIT

Lamson, Wolffe and Company
Boston, New York and London
MDCCCXCVII

The Norwood Press
J. S. Cushing & Co. — Berwick & Smith
Norwood, Mass., U.S.A.

TO

MY MOTHER

"It having pleased the Almighty Ruler of the Universe to defend the cause of the United American States, and finally, to raise us up a powerful friend among the princes of the earth, to establish our liberty and independence upon a lasting foundation, it becomes us to set apart a day for gratefully acknowledging the Divine goodness and celebrating the important event. . . . Upon a signal given, the whole army will huzza, *Long live the King of France!* The artillery then begins again and fires thirteen rounds ; this will be succeeded by a second general discharge of the musketry in a running fire, and huzza, *Long live the friendly European Powers!* The last discharge of thirteen pieces of artillery will be given, followed by a general running fire, and huzza, *The American States!*"

"GEORGE WASHINGTON."

Mademoiselle de Berny

Chapter I

ON an afternoon in early May, in the year
1778, four people rode into the court-
yard of the Green Tree coffee-house in new
Philadelphia, and, dismounting, entered the dining-room. It was a long room poorly lighted
by diamond-paned Dutch casements of greenish
glass set high in the wall and swung half-open.
In the furthest corner from the door lounged
a man, evidently a hanger-on of the place.
His huge bulk clad in drab Quaker costume
was so vaguely defined as to suggest merely a
lightening of the shadow at that particular spot.
His head was dropped on his breast; his legs
stretched out stiffly suggested imminent danger
of his slipping from the bench to the floor. A
red glow showed fitfully beneath the ashes of
his carelessly held pipe.

At the opposite end of the room was the
fireplace of such great width one might look
up the broad-mouthed chimney to the sky.
The backlog was a hewn stone; the blue til-
ing had been brought from Liverpool. Above

the chimney-hood was a carelessly hung painting of George III. of England, in a tarnished
oval frame.

Of the newcomers, one, a British officer,
rose from the chair in which he had seated
himself and, crossing the room, straightened
the picture.

"Such reverence do these knaves pay their
king," he said, "'tis small wonder they do not
turn the portrait clean around and have His
Gracious Majesty a-dancing on his head!"

The one woman of the party, a young girl,
glanced up from the flowers she was arranging.

"Your frown is stupendous, Uncle Henry,"
she said.   "Methinks my words rang true for
all your stormy denial."

Augmented by the mischievous gleaming of
her eyes, the sweetness of her voice seemed
mocking.

"Now, by your honest soul, dear uncle,
confess the truth. You are troubled that these
Provincials prove so well their blood-relation
to His Majesty's troops? But yesterday, I
heard that when the back is turned the towns-
folk whisper 'tis Philadelphia has captured the
British, and not the British Philadelphia."

The little man, still standing near the portrait, made an irritated gesture.

"Do ye wonder, Diane?" he asked; "lo,
have I not known how the dolts smile and

murmur? And this Mischianza," he fumed.
"'Tis well enough for women-folk! They
must have their fol-de-rols. But men, men
I say, turned milliners and dancing-masters,
wearing uniforms as puppet-soldiers. Was't
in this fashion, I ask ye, His Majesty's soldiers were taught to conduct a campaign — to
lie idle the entire winter, gambling and carous-
ing, dancing attendance on these American
belles, who, I warrant ye, laugh in their sleeves
at the young popinjays!"

A young Philadelphian, named Heyward,
seated beside Mademoiselle de Berny on the
bench, which, starting from the fireplace, ran
around the room, had been leaning forward,
his cheek resting on his hand, as he idly trailed
the lash of his riding-whip along the floor.
He drew himself up now, leaning against the
wainscoting, which formed the back of the
seat, shelving out at the top into a ledge for
mugs and pipes.

"Rumor has it that the winter hardships
have but served to toughen the rebels at Valley
Forge," he said, still toying with the whip.
"A hungry dog holds fastest to a bone."

"I warrant ye," retorted General Stirling,
"and a night's march would limber up these
young coxcombs quicker than dancing. Bah,
I can scarce stomach the sight of their smirk-
ings and tip-toeings, and a-picking up the
handkerchiefs of these Whig dames!"

He seated himself at the massive oak table
in the centre of the room, drumming impatiently on the board with his fingers. His
disturbed feeling passed into contentment as he
watched the young girl. To him her hands
appeared even more flower-like than the fragile
blossoms she lifted stem by stem. In the half-
dusk of the room the flowers acquired an intense and delicate whiteness contrasting with
the subdued richness of coloring in her costume. Though bright, the afternoon was cool,
and she had worn over her riding-habit a
cardinal, an article of attire much affected by
the women of those days. This garment, of
crimson satin and fur-trimmed, she had un-
clasped and flung back from her shoulders so
that it made a luxurious setting for her fair
person. Under his bristling brows the soldier's small, irate eyes softened as he watched
her. The fortune of war, he mused, verily, it
was strange. What rude and freakish wind
had blown this blossom to his protection?
He was a rough soldier, unused to the way of
delicate women. A girl's fancy was an uncertain thing — as a bird's flight. Yet, who
could foretell? Perhaps, when the war was
over, and these rebel dogs had been put down
with a strong hand, it would content her to
return with the lad and him to the quiet English home, to be as his daughter in his old age.
And so amidst thought of the turmoil of war—

ay, despite the throbbing of an old wound
in his shoulder — there slipped this day-
dream.

"Your posies are drooping soon, Diane," he
said, his eyes resting kindly upon her.

"They are wild flowers," she answered. She
looked up through the open casement where a
loosened tendril of a vine swayed against the
blue sky. A bird flashed by in the sunlight,
and with a little circling motion sank upon its
nest built in a network of the Virginia creeper
which clambered heavily over the opposite wall
of the court. Her eyes grew dreamy, her face
softening and losing its alert brightness of expression.

"There is an orchard in France," she said
softly, "so old that the trees are gnarled and
bent and bear little fruit; yet, where the
ground slopes downward, runs a stream, so
that the grass all around is long and wet, and
the fleur-de-lis is now in bloom. Sometimes
there were yellow blossoms among the purple,
and some were white, were they not, Armand,"
she asked, addressing a lad who had perched
himself on the further end of the table, one leg
doubled under him, his free foot resting lightly
on the head of a Danish hound crouched upon
the floor. He had been playing on a flute, but
so plaintively sweet and delicate was his music
that although often continuous, it did not disturb conversation, having in its quality some-

thing of the nature of a flower's perfume of which one may be often but half-conscious.

He turned at his sister's question.

"I know, Diane," he nodded. "I could find them sooner than you. The scent of white flowers is stronger."

He slipped down from the table and put his flute away.

"Stir yourself, Little Brother," he said, shoving the hound with his foot. "Come, bestir yourself, great Lazybones," he added as the animal stretched itself, yawning; "will you be forever a-nodding off to sleep like an old dame in a chimney-corner?"

With his hand resting caressingly on the head of the Great Dane, who walked beside him, the lad strolled with a peculiarly hesitating and yet direct step towards his sister. He was a picturesque and slender figure wearing the garb of a mourner. This sable color was relieved only by his ruffled shirt of cambric and lace, and the massive silver buckles at his knees and on his low shoes. At his side dangled a heavy sword in a worn sheath. His ash-yellow hair, lightly powdered, was worn in a queue.

Mademoiselle de Berny rose and with her handkerchief brushed away some of the powder which had drifted upon his coat.

"Don't, Diane," he cried, jerking away; "you can't make a French dandy out of me. It is not I who take after that side of the family."

He drew forth his sword and ran his fingers lightly down the blade, the bright surface of which was spotted as with rust or blood.

"Ah, Diane," he mocked, "'tis I have other blood in me." He stood in the attitude of a listener, his head inclined slightly forward. The merriment in his face did not appear in his eyes, which, large and light gray in color, remained expressionless. In them the diamond-shaped panes of the casement above were reflected as from some glassy surface. He had been blind from birth. His sister not replying, he laughed, and returned the sword to the sheath. The same strong family type was revealed in both faces, although the two were but half brother and sister. With the exception of the coloring, for the girl's hair and eyes bespoke her French nationality, their features were alike save that the oval of her face appeared longer in the lad and his eyes were set nearer together. But in each the high head, the handsome profile, and the full and beautiful curves of the mouth were similar. Even the vein which ran like some faint tracing adown Mademoiselle de Berny's left temple and cheek found its prototype in her brother's face.

"Methinks mine host slower than Father Time," grumbled General Stirling; "a fine country this which chokes one with dust at every step of his horse. Ye have no such vile roads in England. There the dew lies on the green, and good ale flows plenteously."

But as he spoke, the door opened and a negro entered with the tray.

"Were I an American," said Mademoiselle de Berny, seating herself at the table, "my fondness for tea would prove me no rebel."

General Stirling emptied at a draught the mug of ale placed in front of him.

"Don't trouble your pretty head about the rebels!" he said, wiping the foam from his lips. "I fear I am a gruff keeper for so dainty a bird. War is a hard mistress. She does not make ladies' men of us, lily-fingered. We who have grown old in her service know whereof we speak. I remind me of a surgeon once saying that the constant sight of suffering did not harden him, but on the contrary, made it a sorrier thing for him to witness pain, pain which he necessarily gave. So with war. After the pomp and glory prove hollow and the heyday of youth is past, then comes the realization of war. Desolate homes and a waste country, fatherless children and women weeping —" he put his elbow on the table and rested his head on his hand. "I am an old war-horse, my little girl, an old war-horse, who in time of peace is stupid and to be roused only by the scent of battle. Life is a hard lesson. We who fight must not look back over the field, lest our heart sicken."

Mademoiselle de Berny's brother had been leaning on the back of her chair.

"No, no, Uncle Henry," he cried, "war is glorious! Did not my father say, there was fame? Ah, why could not the good God have let him live? I should enlist if Diane would let me. She said they would not take a boy. But you can't fool me, Diane. It is because I am blind."

She put up her hand, covering his as it rested on her shoulder.

"In what capacity could you serve, dear," she asked. "Certainly not in action on the field, and I know of but one other. You would not be a spy, Armand?"

"Why not," said the lad, his face clouding. "What do women know of war? Let go my hand." He slipped into a chair between her and his uncle.

The young man who had been seated beside Mademoiselle de Berny on the bench had not changed his position, engrossed in untying a knot he had made in the lash of his riding-whip. He looked up smiling at the boy's words, directing his amused glance toward the young girl. He rose leisurely and, drawing a chair up to the table, seated himself beside her and opposite General Stirling and his nephew.

"I fear your temper is too frank, my lad," he said pleasantly, "for you to win success as a spy. It takes a less honest man, I fear, to serve in that position."

Young Stirling's mouth quivered with pitiful responsiveness, but he did not speak.

"Trouble not, boy," said his uncle, slapping him on the shoulder; "your spirit is worth a dozen of these hired Hessian louts. Ye'll be called on in good time to serve your king."

Mademoiselle de Berny smiled. "But not as a spy," she said.

"Tut, tut, Diane," said the soldier; "'tis not for a chit of a girl to set up as a judge. Good men and true have entered the secret service. In that particular I hold myself no whit more virtuous than the spy I employ, for do I not benefit by him?"

"I have thought differently," she answered gravely; "always have I been taught that a spy is a necessary evil of war, an instrument whose usefulness cannot veneer its hatefulness and which burns the fingers of those who touch it."

General Stirling shook his head. "Ye show an ungentle heart for a young girl," he frowned.

"The world does not commiserate traitors," she retorted, "at least —"

"You are mistaken there, Mademoiselle," interrupted Heyward, his pleasant face acquiring a shade of earnestness; "a spy is no traitor who betrays his cause. A spy, be he loyal, meeting an ignominious death is a martyr."

"Perhaps," she said, shrugging her shoulders slightly as she passed him a plate of biscuit; "yet a martyrdom scarcely the choice of a gentleman. You agree with me, Monsieur?"

"In war, Mademoiselle," he answered, "men use the term 'patriot' in preference to that of gentleman."

She smiled. In the fashion of the day she held daintily in her fingers the lump of sugar, then accounted a great luxury, with which to sweeten her tea. She took tiny bites of the sugar, sipping the fragrant beverage. Her glance met Heyward's curiously over the cup lifted to her lips.

"In peace," she said, returning the cup to the saucer, "the term 'gentleman' is permitted but one signification, that of a man of honor, but war licenses much, and the word 'patriot' like the mantle of charity covers a multitude of — let us say 'gentlemen' of divers employment. Do I grasp your meaning, Monsieur?"

On the young man's face, habitually grave, with dark eyes over whose intense gaze the lids seldom drooped, dawned a smile. A warm light came into his glance.

"There are some women, Mademoiselle," he said, "whose perfection is such that to disagree with them seems not only a reflection upon a man's gallantry, but even makes his opinion seem wrong because adverse to theirs. And of this argument what shall I say? That neither of us are, perhaps, in a position to render fair judgment? Yet, doubtless, we can both conceive of circumstances in which a patriot would serve his country gladly, in no matter how ignominious a way, and, although it seems paradoxical, yet maintain his honor. After all, why should he be condemned more than the great body of soldiers fighting for the same result?"

"One is permitted to show preference for individuals," she said.

His expression relaxed momentarily into a smile, but he leant a little forward with some eagerness.

"Does not the end sometimes justify the means? A selfish motive only condemns the spy. Otherwise he may hold himself invulnerable. No accusation stings a quiet conscience." His even voice gained a penetrating quality and his eyes burned steadily in an otherwise impassive countenance.

"Think you it a trivial thing for a man to give his life to his country? But if he goes further and lays down that counted dearer than life, his reputation as a man of honor among honorable men? Is it a little thing to forego the glory of a death on the field amongst the foremost, to endure the meanness of a spy's life? And I have always held it the duty of that man, whosoever he is, to serve where he is most needed, and if it lies with him to best perform a peculiar service necessary to the good of his country, he should do it regardless of rank.".

"Bravo! sir," cried the soldier, hitting the table with his fist; "you stir my sluggish blood anew. But how falls it ye wear the garb of a citizen? And, by my faith, ye seem no coward! Fie on ye, young sir, is it by such passive loyalty ye serve your king?"

"I can hold neither party entirely blameless," said Heyward; "still my sympathies incline —"

"Yet sit not idle sucking your thumbs, man," interrupted the other. "It shows more manhood to strike for the party nearest right in your estimation, e'en though it be with the rebels, and I say it as should not, being loyal to King George."

Young Stirling had been leaning across the table whispering to his sister. He laughed, nodding his head, as she refilled his cup of tea. He raised the cup high, the liquid splashing over.

"As good Englishmen," he cried, "we will pledge the health of King George and drink to the downfall of the Boston tea-party."

"Best let the nerve-destroying stuff alone," said General Stirling, gulping down his portion with a wry face.

"Has every one his tea, now?" asked the boy. "Pass me the sugar and a spoon,— a spoon, Diane."

" In a moment, Armand," she answered. As she passed a cup of tea to Heyward, it slipped between their extended fingers, and, hitting against the table-edge, fell broken on the floor.

Mademoiselle de Berny rose, gathering the train of her riding-habit from the spreading liquid.

" There is no tea left, now, Monsieur," she said, " so you cannot drink the toast." She smiled slightly. But though her eyes met his indifferently, her face had grown curiously pale.

General Stirling rose and opened the door, letting a flood of sunlight into the sombre room. He stepped out into the court-yard to order the horses. The kitchen was on the further side of the yard, opposite the dining-room. Thin white-washed pillars ran in a line by house, kitchen, and stable alike, supporting the verandah of the former two and the first floor of the latter. The walls of red and black brick in their checker-board regularity suggested the staid Quaker. Through the archway in the low wall opposite the stable could be seen the street and the varying forms of people passing by. A vine climbed over this wall, wreathing the arch heavily in green. The officer sauntered towards the stable, his pompous little figure in its scarlet uniform brilliant in the mellow sunlight of the latening afternoon.

In the dining-room, Richard Heyward leant against the table, watching Mademoiselle de Berny as she drew on her gloves.

Young Stirling at the further end of the room was feeding biscuit to his dog. He moved back against the man sleeping in the corner, who had changed his position but slightly since the party had entered the room, and then only to relapse into seemingly deeper slumber.

" I beg your pardon, sir," said the lad, bowing with a fine and marked courtesy.

A heavily drawn breath was his only reply.

He waited a moment. Then he stretched out his hand and passed it delicately over the great body and the face with its closed lids and open mouth.

" Your foolish large mouth argues more body than wit, friend," chuckled the lad, slowly withdrawing his hand from the man's cheek.

The eyes of the sleeper opened and shot a quick glance at the boy.

Like a flash young Stirling's hand covered the man's eyes and felt the lashes brush his fingers as the lids closed again. He bent his beautiful face down so that his breath stirred the other's hair.

" A-a-h, my friend," he said, laughing softly and speaking in a whisper, " you were not asleep."

Chapter II

THE other two occupants of the room were oblivious to the incident, the young man being engrossed in buttoning one of Mademoiselle de Berny's gloves, while she was observing him as he did so with an intent gaze which took in every detail of his costume from his brown hair unpowdered and tied with a ribbon, to the boutonnière she herself had pinned on the lapel of his bottle-green coat, made high-collared and with gilt buttons; the full lace ruffles at his breast and wrists; his buff cassimere breeches and high riding-boots. He, growing conscious of her attentive regard, glanced up inquiringly.

"Monsieur," she said, in answer to his unspoken question, "I cannot help wondering why a man whose sentiments are so fine and patriotic should wear citizen's dress and make no effort to prove his valor as a soldier. Your words sounded curiously in my ears as well as in General Stirling's."

His head was bent low over her wrist, but she saw the color rise to the roots of his hair.

"You are very hard on me, Mademoiselle," he said, with a slight protesting laugh; "have

you yet to learn 'tis man's weakness to profess
much that, Spartan-like, you would force him
to prove his words by deeds? Alas, how
clumsy a man's fingers!" he added lightly,
"how fine a woman's veriest trifle! There's
another button gone, but have patience a moment longer."

"A man may profess much, intending little,"
she said, "but I do you no such injustice.
You spoke in no half-hearted fashion, but
bravely, this afternoon. Yet when a citizen
gives to patriotic sentiment such a tone of
feeling, one says, ah, a soldier at heart, but on
which side?"

She felt a tremor run through his fingers.
He had buttoned her glove, but still held her
wrist.

"Monsieur," she continued, "how was it
that when I passed you the cup of tea this
afternoon, your fingers slipped and the tea
was lost? You know what people say — that
no upright loyalist refuses to pledge the health
of his king in tea."

He dropped her wrist, and lifting his head,
met her glance.

"And how does that concern me, Mademoiselle?" he asked, his mouth settling into hard
lines.

"To this extent, Monsieur," she said, "to
this extent." She looked around the room.
In his corner the Quaker had taken an atti-

c

tude of profounder slumber, putting his feet
and legs up on the bench and drawing his hat
over his eyes.   On the further side of the
table, her brother sat on the bench, feeding
cake to his hound.   Then her gaze returned
to Heyward.   In their acquaintance he had
been puzzled by certain unaccountable changes
in her manner from ease and gaiety to coldness
and annoyance.   Now it seemed as if that feeling, which had hitherto shown itself in fitful
bursts of anger and little sparkles of irritation,
had suddenly broken bounds and flamed forth
with the force of a burning challenge.

"Tell me," she said, lowering her tone,
"tell me, why I have not the right to refuse
to associate with one who —" the scornful
words trembled unuttered on her lips.

"Monsieur," she continued after a slight
pause, "I spoke of your dress a moment ago.
Why?   Because although it is the attire of a
gentleman, yet worn by you it signifies something less.   Do you think that it needed but
the spilling of the tea to tell me what your
position is?   Ah, Monsieur, I scorn to say it!
It shames me to know that you are here as a
spy!"

Except for the death-like pallor which
spread over his face, he showed no emotion.

"Do you desire to insult me, Mademoiselle
de Berny?" he said coldly.   His face was set
in a calm which would not be disturbed, but

beneath the lids, as he looked down at her, his eyes seemed a line of gleaming light, cold and suspicious.

As she met his glance, his changed glance, in which hitherto she had read all warmth and trust, her face flamed with passionate anger.

"Insult you," she echoed stingingly, "insult you! Ah, Monsieur, doubtless your position leads you to forget there are those who are generally considered to have lost the right to resent an affront."

He turned and walked towards the half-open door, seeking to maintain his composure.

Mademoiselle de Berny's eyes followed him wrathfully. Her mouth quivered, and the anger in her eyes gave way to pride deeply wounded. She went towards him to go into the court-yard. He, divining her intention, stepped back, opening wide the door, bowing profoundly as she passed him. She did not vouchsafe him a glance. On the verandah she turned and looked back past him into the room where her brother still remained. He had thrown himself lengthwise wearily on the bench and appeared to be sleeping. As she observed his fair hair, his slender form clothed in the mourning garments he could not be persuaded to discard since his father's death over a year ago, her face softened magically.

"Armand," she called gently, "Armand," waiting to see that he heard her, "we must go."

Then as he sat up, stretching his arms and yawning, she turned and went down the steps as the groom brought up her horse.

Heyward watched her hungrily, his heart torn by conflicting emotions. Her horse bent its head to a lump of sugar she held in her palm, and which during lunch she had taken from the table and slipped in the pocket of her cardinal for it. The extravagance of the action at that time, when sugar was accounted a luxury even by the very rich, filled him with bitter resentment. The incident, trifling though it was, yet seemed to separate them more surely than the words which had just passed between them. What comprehension had she of the suffering and oppression which drove men to endure famine and cold for liberty — she, to whom life signified naught save beauty and pleasant ease? Long shadows of the departing day lay across the little court, but did not touch her upon whose slender figure the brightness of the afternoon seemed to be concentrated. Her plumed hat shaded her face so that he could see but the rounded chin, the curving lips, as vividly crimson as the cardinal hanging loosely from her shoulders. Against the rich satin the gray fur trimming of the garment acquired an electrical silvery lustre. And as all that was lovely and to be desired centred in her, so also did it seem to him that he stood in the shadow of whatever was ignoble and to

be despised in the estimate of men. Now he
felt himself under a ban of contumely which
not even her hands, although they should be
extended to him, might push aside.

"Hasten, young sir," cried General Stirling,
impatiently, "are ye gone o' day-dreaming?
What o' the lad, Diane? But here he comes,"
he added, as his nephew emerged from the interior, his hands in his pockets, whistling, the
sun shining full in his unwinking, sightless eyes.

Heyward reëntered the room to procure
his gloves and hat, which, with his riding-whip,
lay on the table near the mass of wild flowers
Mademoiselle de Berny had discarded. He
looked at the drooping blossoms a moment,
but did not offer to touch them. With a
heavy sigh he drew forth his handkerchief, — a
letter slipping unperceived from his pocket to
the floor as he did so, — and passed it over his
forehead, on which appeared the cold beads of
perspiration.

After he had left the room a curious scene
was enacted. The Quaker whirled his feet
suddenly off the bench, and rose, stretching
himself. But he moved, as if unconsciously,
toward the letter, until sufficiently near to cover
it by his foot at the next step. As this was
about to happen, young Stirling's dog picked
up the paper. The fellow bent and spoke
coaxingly to the hound, patting its head, and
pulling gently at the letter held between his

teeth. The animal growled angrily. His owner heard and called him, and the dog trotted out of the room, retaining the letter.

In the street outside the archway, Richard Heyward, pleading an engagement, said good-afternoon, and, turning his horse, rode away in the direction opposite to that which was taken by the rest of the party.

"The young man was not gallant, Diane," observed General Stirling, his eyes twinkling. "What did ye to him that he left us in such hasty fashion?"

"I," she answered, "I but asked him a simple question, were the tea I poured too sweet or too bitter that he spilled it, and lo, he frowned as at some sorry jest."

"Ye jest far," said the soldier; "'twas a reflection on the man's honor ye made, Diane. Thy idle words are oft-times barbed."

She laughed. "If the coat fits," she said airily.

"Hark ye, my girl," he said, his shaggy eyebrows drawn together in a heavy frown and raising one hand in emphasis of his words, "lest such careless hinting breathe dishonor on a man's fair name as a breath dims the bright steel."

"But you breathe on a blade," she retorted with a certain arch mischievousness which well became her, "and, but a moment, be the steel good, the mist vanishes."

The soldier smiled, half-resentful, yet wholly charmed. "Ye make poor excuse for an ungentle heart, Diane," he said, shaking his head.

"You are a fussy old dame, dear uncle," she rejoined sweetly, "with your preaching and your scoldings, which like so many concoctions of herbs are excellent but not diverting."

Social life was awakening in Philadelphia after the torpor of the long day.

The shadows of the houses already stretched across the cobble-stone pavement as the little party walked their horses leisurely down Second Street, but above their heads the sky was still deeply blue, and the steep roofs with their quaint pent-eaves and ponderous cornices were touched by the lingering gold of the last sun-rays. On the low front stoops the belles in brocaded gowns, spread to advantage over enormous hoops, were waiting with stately serenity the coming of the beaux. And there were to be seen many sweet and natural faces despite the coquetry of black patches on rose-tinted cheeks and chins and the heads loaded by immense cushions over which was drawn the powdered hair. Their feet in high-heeled slippers and huge buckles were crossed to display the slender ankles. Good loyalists in wigs and smallclothes were meeting in neighborly converse, exchanging the courtesy of the snuff-box and the last choice scandal, passing the news from the mother-country and indulg-

ing in many a witticism at the expense of the
starving rebels at Valley Forge — so many rats
driven into a hole, snarling at the prosperity of
the sleek loyalists. Ay, but they had had a
long winter to cool the white glow of their
fervor!

Frequent glances were cast upon General
Stirling and his companion as they walked
their horses abreast, conversing but little. In
front of them rode the boy, his hound at his
horse's heels. Beside him was an orderly of
the general's, mounted and in close attention
upon the blind rider. Gay young British officers hovering around those stoops where pretty
girls held court, drawn as irresistibly to the
spot as bees to honey, were discussing the fête
to be given in honor of the retiring commander,
Lord Howe, who had been recalled to England.
Never had the citizens of a captive city passed
a winter more gaily social. But the prospective instatement of Sir Henry Clinton menaced
this gaiety, threatening a speedy end. Now for
the first time was attention paid to those
veteran soldiers who, like unpleasant birds of
warning, had croaked the winter through that
the loose discipline of the army was doing more
to weaken it than any battles yet experienced.
Their chagrin at the follies and inaction of the
troops grew greater as certain of the officers
treated as a jest a rebuke which should have
been the keenest mortification. Of these, one

who had most loudly voiced his irritation and
waxed most hotly contemptuous was General
Stirling.   Muttered comments were made and
unfriendly looks cast upon the little man as he
sat stiffly astride his huge gray horse, glancing
seldom either to the left or right, his face set
grim, acknowledging surlily the salutes of the
young officers.

"An army of Miss Nancys," he said, snorting with contempt as he and his companions
drew to one side of the narrow street to make
way for a coach drawn by four horses, and pre-
ceded by outriders.   The coach-horses, milk-
white and gaily caparisoned, trotted briskly
down the street.   In the coach, which had great
bravery of gilding and upholstery, reclined
Lord Howe, the retiring commander.   With
much pleasant bowing did he turn his head
from side to side, his horses slackening into a
walk.   Once did he raise his hat with more
than usual elaborate courtesy as he passed the
former owner of the coach and four, a wealthy
spinster, who had yielded with ill-grace to the
forced lending of her property.   His urbane
bow was returned but sourly by the powdered
dame from the faded sedan chair in which she
was being carried along the sidewalk by slaves.

Although quick to perceive the humor of a
situation, Mademoiselle de Berny did not smile
at this incident, returning Lord Howe's bow
but absently, as he turned towards her and

General Stirling. As the little party continued its way, she drew from her reticule the letter her brother had taken from his dog and given to her to hold for him. The paper, unaddressed and folded to form the envelope, was fastened by black wax, the seal of which she recognized as Richard Heyward's. Her hand trembled. A variety of emotions showed in her countenance, scorn impelling her to toss the paper away; anxiety as she glanced at General Stirling, lest he should be curious of the contents, but he seemed absorbed in deep thought; lastly, a defiant expression which yet revealed an underlying tenderness as she replaced the letter in the reticule.

"Did you read that, Diane?" asked her brother, turning in his saddle.

"No," she answered; "Mr. Heyward must have dropped it."

"Give it back to me, then," he said, stretching out his hand. His horse veered. He felt for the reins, which he had let go for a moment. The orderly had reached over and taken them.

"Let my horse alone, sirrah," cried the boy, his face all aflame. "I granted you permission to ride beside me in case of accident or unsafe road, but I will not be put in leading-strings! My horse obeys me at a word." He gathered the reins in one hand and took his whip in the other.

"This fellow is all Diane's doing," he muttered. "I am no child. Some day I shall teach her a lesson for this." Raising his whip, he struck his horse several times. The animal reared and plunged violently, but its rider had it in superb control.

"There, Diane," he called over his shoulder. "There," hitting his horse again and again, "and there." He, laughing and breathless in his excitement forgot, for the time being, the letter.

Orders were issued in Philadelphia the following day for the arrest of one Richard Heyward, a spy of the Continental Army, hitherto known as a loyalist. Indignation at the accusation was loudly expressed by the friends of the young man. But when it was learned that several days previous he had obtained a passport to go beyond the lines and at nightfall he had not been found, no further proof of his guilt seemed needed.

Mademoiselle de Berny heard the news, her mouth quivering with scorn. So at her words he had turned and fled craven-hearted — a spy fleeing the wrath of honest men. In a brief moment had her whilom lover become an enemy. But a direct question as to his honor, and the cloven hoof had shown. Well, he had escaped. He was in safety, at all events. He had passed out of her life, going without an explanation or a farewell, as a thief in the night. Yet, though

she puzzled long over the fact as to how his
position could have become so quickly known,
she could not bring herself to ask any questions,
dreading with a sensitiveness almost abnormal
to hear any comments made upon his base position and cowardly flight.

The day following this she was destined to receive a still greater shock. The orderly who
accompanied her brother when he rode sought
her in great distress. He was one of the hired
Hessian troops, a faithful, stupid fellow. His
yellow hair was matted to his forehead by perspiration; his round face, red and streaked with
dust from rapid riding, was lined with anxiety.
Young Stirling's horse, whose reins he had
fastened to his own saddle, was riderless. It
appeared that the boy, always indulged in his
fondness for riding in the country, had received
permission from his uncle to go to Frankfort,
a small milling centre, five miles from the city.
Once there, he had dismounted at the Jolly
Post, and bidding the orderly see to the horses,
had given him some money with the injunction
to spend an hour or so in good company, while
he with his dog amused himself sauntering
through the village. The fellow finding right
hearty cheer and good comrades, waited well
content until noon. Then as his young master
did not come, he engaged in a vain search for
him. Several children reported having seen
him and his dog walking rapidly down the

forest road, which was in reality a continuation
of the one village street. The orderly had followed the road some distance, but his search
proving futile, and fearing the approach of
night, he returned to Philadelphia for assistance, having already taken the precaution of
sending some country people to look for the
missing boy. General Stirling and a guard
rode out the Frankfort road, searching high
and low in the vicinity of the village, lighting
torches as it grew darker, advancing a long distance into the wood. To their hallooing there
was no response save the lonely baying of a
farm dog. That the lad had either wandered
far into the forest or been picked up by some
passer-by there could be no doubt.

Mademoiselle de Berny waited in an agony
of suspense at the gateway of the Quaker
house where she resided, her strained gaze
striving to penetrate the darkness at the bend
of the street, from which direction the searching-party would return. A fitful wind was
blowing; the swayings and sighings of the
trees caused her to shiver with apprehension.
High in the heavens the moon appeared
through swiftly moving clouds. Her fears
took the form of wildest imaginings. Now
she saw her brother make a misstep and fall
into the stream; now he ran against a tree,
bruising himself, or he wandered off the road;
perhaps the far worse fate overtook him of

falling into the hands of a band of Tory ma-
rauders, the terror of the country-side. She
could hear him sobbing her name as when a
little child he had awakened in the night and
missed her. So real was his imagined cry that
she put her hands over her ears, moaning. As
she strove to control herself and think clearly,
it seemed to her that his action was not impulsive, but evidently deliberately planned. Her
mind travelled slowly over the events of the
past few days, striving to find some clue to his
conduct. Struck by a sudden thought, she
turned and walked swiftly back to the house,
and entering ascended the stairs to her room.
She opened her desk and touched the spring of
a secret compartment known only to herself
and her brother. The letter she had concealed
there was gone!

The wind blew the white curtains at her
casement fantastically. The little oil lamp on
her dressing-table flared wildly, filling the room
with smoke. But the young girl seated at her
desk, her chin resting in the palms of her hands,
noticed nothing, deep in painful thought, her
gaze fixed on the rifled drawer. The solution
of her brother's escapade was clear to her now.
Armand, in a spirit of adventure, had gone to
Valley Forge, — whither Richard Heyward had
evidently fled, — intent upon returning the letter
to its rightful owner. Now, as an added pang to
her anxiety was the humiliation of knowing that

over Armand as well as herself, Richard Heyward had exerted an irresistible charm, so that
the lad's chief delight had lain in the young
man's society. It seemed an exhibition of this
man's power, an added insolence on his part, as
it were, that her brother should disregard her
to go to him. She pictured Armand, frail and
blind, trudging a lonely road, his faithful hound
at his side, on his errand of loyalty and love to
one who, while gratified at the return of the
letter, was yet amused at the lad's preference —
an echo of the sister's heart! Her powerlessness
was the most torturing humiliation to her.
Could she by any means have wrested Armand
away from Heyward, with whom he probably was,
and have torn the unfortunate letter in pieces —
her hands clinched in helpless resentment and
her eyes filled with burning tears of anger.
There was the trampling of horses' hoofs on
the cobble-stone pavement, growing steadily
louder. She pushed aside the curtains and
leant out of the casement. She saw the weary
searchers, whose dejected attitude, as they walked
their horses up the street, betrayed their failure.
General Stirling dismounted in front of the
house, bidding the rest of the party wait. He
opened the gate into the yard. Mademoiselle
de Berny had almost flown down the stairway
and met him, ere he had advanced half-way up
the flower-bordered walk which led to the
house. As the light from the hallway fell

upon his perturbed and troubled countenance, his scarlet uniform covered with dust and still damp from a light rain which had fallen early in the evening ; the gold lace torn ; above all, his hand lacerated by the broken limb of a tree, — she realized how serious and arduous had been his search.   All anger and thought of Heyward were swept away in the renewed flood of anxiety for Armand, which made her solution of his disappearance seem for the moment an absurdity, with a criminal aspect, considering the tragic present.

"There, there," said General Stirling, smoothing her hair with awkward tenderness, as she stood sobbing, her face hidden on his shoulder, her slender arms clasping convulsively his stalwart figure ; "we will find him to-morrow.   I will prove ye then the truth o' my words, that he is in safe keeping.   Ye must not weep so, Diane. It hurts me sorely.   Diane, ye will break my heart to cry so.   My little girl, the boy is safe."

And though the missing lad was his only nephew, and the girl, his niece by courtesy merely, being the step-daughter of his dead brother, yet was he more troubled by her tears than by the boy's absence, and felt an anger which made his kindly face grow stern as he looked at the little mournful head resting on his shoulder.   He had no patience of pranks which caused such weeping, having always a great tenderness for the weakness of women.

Chapter III

VERY early the following morning, while the stars still shone palely, two shadowy figures passed swiftly through the sleeping city. The shorter and stouter of these two figures wore the gray garb and bonnet of a Quakeress. The other was attired in a long drab garment, the hood of which the wearer had pulled well over her head, giving her a cloister-like appearance. The light growing stronger revealed these two women to be Mademoiselle de Berny and Rachel Mott, the latter an elder maiden daughter of the family with whom the young girl and her brother made their home while in Philadelphia.

Mademoiselle de Berny addressed her companion. "You are sure we will be able to pass the line, Rachel?"

"Yea, if thou wilt but say I am thy maid come to carry the flour," answered the other, who bore an empty sack on one arm.

"Give me the passport now," said the young girl, "that I may have it in readiness."

At that time the citizens of Philadelphia were allowed by the British to obtain flour from the Frankfort mills. When, therefore, the previous evening, Rachel Mott, a Quaker-

ess of good standing, had applied at headquarters for license to pass the lines, her request to obtain flour for her family had been
readily granted, although made at a late hour,
it being half after ten o'clock. This permission
had been asked by the Quakeress at the solici-
tation of Mademoiselle de Berny, in whose
nature it was not consistent that she should
long repine when there remained a possibility
of action. Even as she had buried her tear-
wet face on General Stirling's broad breast the
evening preceding, her mind had been busily
cogitating a plan by which she should go in
search of her brother. She had bidden her
guardian good night with an eagerness to have
him go, which was not unmingled with an excess of affection, the warmth of which had its
origin in a secret contrition at the thought of deceiving him. When he had at last taken his departure, she ran swiftly up the stairs to the room
of Rachel Mott, who was preparing to retire,
begging her to dress again and obtain a passport
to go to Frankfort in the morning, stating her
intention to go to the rebels' camp for her
brother. She had found herself at some serious
difficulty in persuading her timid companion to
fall in with her plans, but her stronger will
had prevailed. Moreover, her statements, nay,
threats, that should any misfortune happen to
her brother through her not being at his side
to protect him, the Quakeress would also be

partly responsible, as those are guilty who leave
undone those things which they ought to do,
had the effect of terrorizing into obedience the
meek Friend, whose gentle heart was in a flutter
of trepidation between furthering Mademoiselle's rash venture and her duty, which seemed
to consist in doing this very thing for which she
would later be condemned by the young girl's
guardian. But she was powerless before the
imperious mandate of Mademoiselle de Berny,
who had assisted her to dress, wrapped her
cloak hurriedly around her and almost pushed
her down the stairway and out of the house,
and then awaited impatiently her return from
headquarters with the passport, the ready
granting of which at that late hour could be
laid only to the looseness of discipline which
then marked the condition of the British Army.

While Mademoiselle de Berny had passed
the hours intervening between the settlement
upon their plans for the morrow and the time of
starting in fitful and troubled sleep, the Quakeress had spent the greater part of the night
fervently praying. For to-morrow was there
not to be met General Stirling, when she should
return alone from Frankfort, having left Mademoiselle to continue her unprotected way to
the camp of the ungodly rebels?

"And whilst he would not speak harshly to
his niece," she murmured, "thou knowest, O
Lord, that he is not slow to anger and useth a

violent temper and a profane tongue towards those he loveth not that vex him."

Now she trudged patiently at Mademoiselle's side, her timorous and maidenly soul still doubting and protesting, but saying naught to her companion who pressed on hurriedly, ever a little in advance in her eagerness and anxiety.

The young girl took but little into account the peril which a woman surely courted who ventured to travel alone in the present trouble-some times. Only the peculiar circumstances of her life allowed her to so ignore the rashness of this errand. From the seclusion of a con-vent, she had become one of the gay whirlpool of a licensed and unrestrained court society, which latter condition she had left for the even freer and more changeful environment of army life that her companionship with her step-father, and since his death, with General Stirling, had given her. And in common with her brother she possessed a daring spirit and a love of adventure which caused her rather to invite than to shun peril. So, although she had taken the precaution to wear a Friend's cloak, which was an effectual masque, she had dis-missed any vague thought of personal danger as a matter of secondary importance where Armand was concerned. Upon him she lavished that tenderness of love, which his dead mother might have given, idolizing him, worshipping

his delicacy and beauty, comprehending him
through his likeness to her, ashamed of her
jealousy of his constant thought of his father,
whose death had not made him less to his son,
and yet understanding this faithfulness in the
boy by the very love which made her desires
centre in him.   She felt the dauntless self-reli-
ance women experience when loved ones are in
danger.   This confidence in their own ability,
the desire to take matters into their own hands,
which women have at such times, appears to
spring from the maternal sense of protection,
which ignoring danger to self instinctively feels
the heart the surest loadstone.   And there
were doubtless other motives prompting Mademoiselle de Berny upon this occasion, motives
of which she was unconscious.   She had not
confided her intention of going to Valley Forge
to General Stirling, knowing that he would un-
compromisingly condemn as unfeasible her proj-
ect to follow her brother, and would seek to
reassure her by stating that the searching-party
would again be sent out.   Yet, she knew well
their search would be in vain had Armand
reached the rebel camp.   She, a woman and
alone, would doubtless be permitted to pass the
American lines.   A deeper motive actuated
this secrecy, a motive which she would not
have confessed even to herself, and would have
indignantly denied if accused of possessing.
Her statements of the reasons which led her

to believe that Armand had gone to Valley
Forge would involve the explaining of the
letter, and from this she shrank, recoiling as
one from a touch upon an unhealed wound,
the mention of Richard Heyward.

In the east the dawn was whitening. There
was heard the twitter of waking birds. The
tree-tops swayed in the sharp breeze which is
born just before dawn and dies down. The
young girl shivered, drawing her cloak closely
around her. She looked up. Far above in the
heavens a few stars were still shining, but so
faintly as to be scarcely luminous. As she
lowered her glance she saw that the long line
of light in the east was slowly brightening into
gold. They were nearing the city limits.
Small signs of the day's activities appeared.
As they passed the court-house which stood
on arches built on brick pillars, they caught
glimpses in these arched apertures of venders
arranging their vegetables for the morning
market. From out the cool dusk glimmered
the orange of carrots, the glossy leaves of the
wintergreen with its scarlet berries, bundles
of sassafras bark, potatoes, the gold of sweet
country butter, Indian baskets filled with maple
sugar, deliciously fresh. On the further side
of the street the hucksters' wagons were ar-
rayed in a long row. An old man climbed
painfully the flight of stairs leading to the tiny
balcony over the main entrance of the building.

A moment later and the bell in the little cupola rang out unevenly but sweetly.

"It is five o' the clock," said Rachel Mott.

A milk wagon loomed up grayly, rattling over the cobble-stone pavement. The driver was whistling cheerily. Mademoiselle de Berny called to him, and he drew up his horses close to the curbstone. He was a fresh-cheeked country lad, shrewd eyed, and with a merry smile. At her request he filled the cover of a can with milk for herself and her companion. He refused payment.

"'Tis enough in these days to be asked civilly for a draught of milk," he said. "But yesterday those thieving British rogues, the sentry, helped themselves freely enough to my ware. And the cream! Why, mon, says I to one fellow, do you think it naught but milk, and skimmed at that! Ye should have seen the likes o' them, ma'am! The way that cream, yellow as a buttercup, slipped down their saucy throats! Small thanks to them, says I, that they didn't spill on the ground what they didn't want."

"The British rogues," repeated Mademoiselle de Berny; "are you then a Whig?"

"Eh, no, lady," he answered with a hearty laugh and a sly wink over his shoulder at the Quakeress; "ye'll find me mealy mouthed as any Friend and no such ninny as to answer that question unless ye tell me first which side ye be on."

She smiled. "I have no concern in the matter," she said. "How near the lines are we now?"

He pointed backward with his whip. "A ten minutes' walk straight ahead o' ye."

She paused to inquire if he had any news of her brother. He replied in the negative.

As the two women approached the redoubt, beyond which lay the Frankfort road, Mademoiselle de Berny drew her hood further over her head. She knew the place to be garrisoned by the Queen's Rangers, under the command of an officer with whom she had some acquaintance, and she preferred to pass unrecognized by him, if possible. They saw but the sentry, however, who allowed them to proceed without trouble. A moment later they stepped upon the Frankfort road and received the free sweep of air across the country which was, in general, cleared ground, but intersected by many woods and high fences. From the dark fields rose vaporish mists, winding away like ghosts of the vanished night. The line of gold in the east widened. The tree-tops caught the brightening reflection. Flocks of small clouds became a luminous rose color, moving slowly towards the horizon. The breeze rose briskly, fragrant with the odor of the fresh, damp air and subtly suggestive of country life. Madem-

oiselle de Berny pushed back the hood of her
cloak with a sigh of relief. Her eyes, sombre
from a sleepless night, had the strained expression of one striving to perceive something as
yet beyond the range of vision. She had a
curious fancy that but a few steps further,
a turn of the road, and she should catch a
glimpse of her brother with his dog walking
ahead of her. She found herself hastening
at every curve of the highway, her lips involuntarily forming his name to call to him. And
always when she had passed the turn she
dropped back into a slower pace with a sickening
pang of disappointment, despite the unreason-
ableness of the fancy.

Now country-folk appeared, the goodwife
seated on a pillion behind her husband, holding a basketful of eggs or a firkin of butter, and
always a bright nosegay of hardy garden flowers.
Farmers appeared at intervals, a forlorn set
of men, as they jogged disconsolately along,
their wagons half-empty. In constant danger
of seeing their fields robbed or trampled upon
by cavalry, and in some instances set afire,
they lacked courage to sow anew or to raise
more than a few vegetables.

Of these people Mademoiselle de Berny inquired vainly for news of her brother. On
either side of them stretched the woods, high
rails fencing it from the road. Where some
distance ahead the road made an abrupt turn,

the two women caught a glimpse of horsemen
through the trees and the sparkle and flash of
sunlight hitting upon steel.   The ground trembled.   There was a thundering and increasing
sound of trampling.   The Quakeress drew her
companion quickly to one side of the road
close to the fence.   She was none too soon.
Down the road came a drove of cattle.   Clouds
of dust, golden in the sunlight, rose volumi-
nously as smoke concealing the last of the drove.
But through the dust could be seen the glossy
hides of black cattle and red and white of
another breed.   There were about a hundred
head, sleek and well fed.   When they had
passed, and the dust had settled slightly, there
appeared some little distance behind a party of
British cavalry, laughing and talking in a gale
of good spirits.   The two women recognized
them as belonging to the Queen's Rangers, a
corps of native American loyalists drawn from
Connecticut.   A brave showing they made in
the fresh morning, all young and stalwart men,
their horses black or roan and their uniforms a
clear fine green, in color like unto those worn
by Robin Hood and his men in the old forest
of Sherwood.   These uniforms put on at the
close of winter, as the earth took on its
spring-like garb of green, would by autumn
have nearly faded with the leaves, retaining
their most desirable characteristic of being
scarcely discernible at a distance.   The com-

manding officer drew rein, inquiring of the
Quakeress if he could be of any assistance to
her and her companion, glancing sharply as he
spoke at Mademoiselle de Berny who stood
with averted head, her hood drawn so closely
as to well-nigh conceal her countenance. At
the Quakeress' simple explanation that they
were on their way to procure flour at Frankfort, he permitted them to proceed without
further question. They had gone but a little
way, however, when they heard the galloping
of a horse behind them. The officer, leaving
his men standing, had ridden back to offer the
services of one of his soldiers to carry the bag
on his saddle back to Philadelphia, as it would
doubtless be heavy. As he spoke his gaze was
fixed with undisguised curiosity and almost suspicion upon Mademoiselle's shrouded figure,
whose face he could not see, but the distinction of whose bearing illy concealed by the
Quaker garment convinced him that this was
no ordinary personage, but a gentlewoman who
wore the cloak as a disguise, and the profession
on whose part of such an errand was odd, even
calculated to raise suspicion in those Philadelphian days, when the fine ladies were carried
in sedan chairs, and who called a slave to pick
up the handkerchiefs they dropped. But his
curiosity was baffled as the Quakeress again replied that she was the maid come to carry the
flour and that the sack would be light weight.

He asked to see their passport, however, and examined it carefully, returning it without comment and, bidding them good morning, rejoined his party.

Beyond a rustic bridge spanning a creek, on a wooded height, they could see the village of Frankfort. It was seven o'clock when they reached it.

" Do you know, Rachel," said Mademoiselle de Berny, as they reached the top of the hill, panting from the exertion of climbing, " I feel always as if I were part of a picture when I come here and had none other reality than a figure in the landscape. It makes me think of the German towns across the water. Ah, Rachel, how it saddens me. What joy is there to me in pictures when Armand cannot see ? "

The little Quakeress, mild eyed and gentle as a dove, her rapid breathing fluttering the white kerchief crossed over her breast, answered with up-raised eyes : " Knowest thou not, Diane, that the Good Book saith that the lust of the flesh and the lust of eyes and the pride of the flesh is not of God, but of the world ? Bethink thee of those who have eyes yet see not. How sad is that. Oft have I heard it said by reverend and elderly people that the afflicted are those favored of the Lord."

Mademoiselle de Berny looked down into the honest eyes of her companion —the blue and simple eyes which seemed but to mirror

holy thoughts. She put her own arm around
the gray-clad shoulders, and laid her cheek a
moment against the Quakeress'. "Rachel,"
she said, "you are ten years older than I, yet
you are as a little child. But I am not so
blessed. You are so good that your prayers
will avail more than mine. Pray we shall find
him soon. No, no, Rachel; not a word!
Waste no time in speech, nor even pause to
think, but pray; pray as heartily as if 'twere
the salvation of your own soul you sought;
and I," she added laughing, "will look out for
the things of this world; but you cease not
to pray, or I shall do you an ill-turn for it,
Rachel."

Along the one street which formed the village were clumps of cherry and plum trees
wrapped in the fragrant white mist of their
blossoms. Here and there a peach tree blew
pink in blossom, like a blush of spring. Grass
grew in the street. Business was at a stand-
still. Now and then they passed fences and
rails which had been torn up and made into
temporary huts for soldiers, but were now deserted. The houses were low and built of
stone. The doors, divided into two parts,
were mostly closed, although it was not overly
early in the morning. They passed a house
in which the upper part of the door was open,
the lower half closed to keep the domestic animals from running into the house. Appear-

ing in the upper half, as a picture in a frame, a contemplative German, smoking a pipe, nodded good morning to them. A dog barked at their heels. As they drew near the end of the village they heard the cheery clacking of the wheel and the splashing of the mill-stream. The miller, a stout, florid fellow, his blouse and hair powdered with flour, informed Mademoiselle de Berny that a boy and a dog, answering her description, had paused at the mill yester morning, asking the way to the rebels' camp up the Schuylkill. He had then crossed the little mill-stream at the ford further down a few steps. Yes, some soldiers had inquired for him. Blind? He had not noticed. But now that he thought of it, he recollected the strange look o' the lad's eyes. Some one, a Quaker, he judged from the broad-brimmed hat and drab clothes, met him away down the road, beyond the stream. The lad had a pleasant way. He was her brother, perhaps, only his skin was fairer. And his hair he had observed, because it was the color of his own little daughter's — the tint o' corn when it was near to ripening.

The Quakeress seated herself wearily on a bench near the door, but Mademoiselle de Berny stood looking over the stream with troubled eyes. The sunlight fell on her slender figure and her sad face.

"I shall go after him, Rachel," she said; "I

am confident he has reached the American camp, or we should have heard of him ere this. He probably fell in with some Quaker going that way, I should judge, from what this good man tells us. When you return to Philadelphia explain my absence to General Stirling. Avoid seeing him until late in the afternoon, so he can force no information from you. Then it will not avail him to send for me, as I will be within the rebel lines. Tell him kindly, Rachel, that I thought it wisest, and give him my most dutiful love."

"But, my child," interposed the little Quakeress, "thou art rash to run into such danger. Thou art young, and I say not falsely that thou hast the comeliness of the flesh which warreth against the spirit. No one will harm the boy, and it would be wise that thou return with me, would it not?" glancing appealingly at the miller.

The joint advice of the two availed nothing.

"And thou hast not yet broken fast save by a sup of milk," pleaded the Quakeress; "thou wilt grow faint on the way. Do thou harken, Diane, lest thy ungodly self-will lead thee into wrong paths."

"The Lord prospers them as begin the day on a full stomach," said the miller. His jovial face beamed with good nature. He pointed to a stone cottage back of the mill, well-nigh hidden by fruit trees. "Go in and have some-

thing with the goodwife. I but just left the
little ones around the table a-blowing of their
porridge to cool it. Six sound boys have I
and a little daughter, who the old mothers say
is the image o' her father." He shook with
silent merriment.

But Mademoiselle de Berny would not con-
sent to tarry longer, being sorely harried by
fear lest she should be delayed, her thought
reverting to the suspicious attitude taken by
the officer they had encountered.

"Rachel," she said, a smile belying the anxiety in her eyes, "why dwell you so on the
bodily pleasures of eating? Have you no
shame of your appetite? Take care," she
added, shaking her head, and with droll mim-
icry of the other's voice, "lest your ungodly
desires lead you to lust for the flesh-pots of
Egypt, and you sell your birthright for a mess
of pottage!"

Nodding her head as in solemn prophecy of
things unspeakably awful, Rachel Mott watched
her companion fording the stream, her dress
gathered closely around her slender ankles,
the light twinkling on the buckles of her
slippered feet, as she stepped daintily from
stone to stone with the miller's assistance.
On the further side of the stream Mademoiselle
de Berny turned.

"Adieu," she cried, waving her hand, "your
solemn face does make me merry, Rachel.

Faith, I would wager a pair of gloves you think me on the road to a warmer world; but fear not, I shall be back in time for the ball, and I will wear my butterfly gown. Who knows but the tempter may whisper you to join in the dance for all your pious garb?"

"Ah, Diane," murmured the Quakeress, as she awaited the miller's return to procure the flour, "the heathenish name thy parents gave thee suits thee right well, and with good sense didst thou choose thy costume for dancing — that invention of the devil's! Thy frivolous French blood makes thee indeed a butterfly! Take heed lest thy pretty wings be singed."

As some dove whose fellows have flown away, leaving it alone, sunning its gentle bosom, so did the little Quakeress seem, seated on the bench, with the distressed tears falling on the white kerchief which crossed her breast. For there was the misery of the thought of Mademoiselle de Berny in danger, and there remained General Stirling, whose wrath she must encounter.

"And whilst he would not speak harshly to his niece," she murmured, "because of her French airs and graces, which exercise a most ungodly influence, so that her disobedient heart is not to be perceived for the glamour of her way, yet 'tis known how violent a temper and profane a tongue he useth towards them that cross him."

E

Chapter IV

"FOUR miles yonder," said the miller, "following the road straight, ye pass the Red Lion Tavern, which is at a cross-roads, and there ye take the path to your left. Or ye can cut across country through the forest, which is a lonesome way, but makes better time. I'll show ye another bit if ye go that way, though 'tis scarce to my liking to see ye go alone in these rough times. Yet ye tell o' the poor lad's blindness, and I marvel not that ye are fearsome for him." He swung open the gate of the fence, which railed in a pasture from the road, flapping his white apron to drive away the curious cows. A footpath led across this meadow to a dense woods. Mademoiselle de Berny walked swiftly, her companion puffing and blowing as he kept pace with her. The flour which had settled upon his blue blouse and his hair rose with every step, making in the sunlight a radiant nimbus around his red face and portly figure. As he was about to leave her on the border of the forest, after pointing out the path, Mademoiselle de Berny put a tiny blue ring she had been wearing in his broad palm. "Take that to your little daughter," she said, "and when I return, either to-night or to-morrow morning, I shall partake of some porridge with her."

The miller stood a moment watching her. Beneath the glimmer of the green trees her figure, clad in the long cloak and pointed brown hood, had a quaint, unworldly appearance, as of a nun, whose convent walls were made by the close forest. But as she turned to wave a last adieu to him, this fancy was dispelled; for no holy face looked out from beneath the pointed hood, but a countenance brilliant in color, with mischievous gleaming eyes and escaping curls clustering around the delicate forehead, and half-concealing the dainty pink of the ears.

"Good morning, my friend," she called, "fail not to tell Rachel Mott that with your own eyes you saw me fall into the clutches of the Evil One!"

Now, though Mademoiselle de Berny walked on bravely the road the miller pointed out, her steps at last became hesitating. She felt as one who has wandered into an enchanted wood. Trees arose on all sides, their branches interlacing gloom of verdure the sun-rays could barely penetrate. Branches lay broken on the ground. Now and then she stepped over the great trunk of some fallen forest king covered with fungi and moss. It was still in the cool of the morning. The dew lay white as hoar-

frost on the ground.   A red squirrel ran across
her path.   Through a far gap in the forest,
where the sunshine streamed down broadly,
there passed in single file a long line of Indians
with feathered head-dress, their supple bodies
glistening like copper.   She stood still watching them stealing away like wood-spirits.   Her
eyes grew wide and dark, seeming to reflect in
their depth the mysteriousness of the forest.
There arose the lonely cooing of a dove.   It
seemed to her that the heart of the woods was
voicing its longing.   She thought of a picture
hanging in the dormitory of a convent she had
attended — The Enchanted Wood.   Again she
saw the little painted spring, in which the fairies
bathed, bubbling from the moss.   Pleasant had
it been to imagine herself wandering through
those elf-like glades on carpets of rarest moss
underneath the arching of great trees.   Ah,
how this place brought back those fairy-tales —
all those dreams of her childhood never to be
realized !   Yet had one dream, that of being in
such a forest, come to pass.   Here was the
spring and the velvet moss and the gigantic
trees.   But as the morning brightened into day,
she would fain have turned and fled.   For so
it is with mankind, beauty taking on the color
of the mood.   For though the supreme desire
be fulfilled, it proves an empty shell, turning
to ashes and bitterness if those beloved have
no part in it.

Mademoiselle de Berny's thought drifting to
the quaint saying that souls were oft-times lone-
liest in Paradise, felt as if the beauty choked
her. Beneath her anxiety regarding her brother
ran an undercurrent of thought of Richard
Heyward. Crossing the ocean to this far
country had there not been a sweet and secret
hope nestling as some hidden singing-bird in
her breast? And while he had forgotten that
brief meeting in far off France, she had remembered! She put her hands over her burning
face. Since his cowardly flight from Philadelphia, branded shamelessly in public opinion as
a spy, her scorn of his base position and her
wounded pride that he had left her without a
word had kept her thought at a tension which
allowed no play of the emotions. But a great
rush of sadness now swept away all anger and
pride, leaving her powerless against the cry of
her heart for him. Certain gestures — the car-
riage of his head, the lighting of his face when
he smiled, the warmth which had come into his
glance when he looked at her — now became
torturing remembrances. Within her tender
heart, beneath all surface anger, there throbbed
the ever ready pardon for him when he should
come back to her and be forgiven — not for-
giveness in the common acceptance of the term,
but rather the assurance the passionate and generous nature would convey to the beloved one
that what has passed is as naught. She felt

the humbleness of the forgiver craving pardon,
that he should be right rather than the other.
In the quiet forest there was heard the sound
of weeping.   Mademoiselle de Berny seated on
the trunk of a tree, her head bowed upon her
knees, was sobbing as if her heart would break.
Love she felt had come to her, not as a flame
to purify even as it burned, nor yet a sharp
pain which might chasten, never an inspiration,
but hopeless and a grievous hurt, a sore, slight
perhaps, but unhealing, throbbing at the source
of being, lying deeper than any trouble she had
ever known.   With a pang of self-reproach she
remembered Armand and rising, continued her
way, walking with conscience-stricken haste to
make up for lost time.   In her hurry she forgot the miller's direction to be followed at the
cross-roads some distance before the Red Lion
Tavern would be reached, and took the wrong
path.   This way wound circuitously through
the forest so that it was nearly noon before she
passed from the woods into the open country.
The highway lay white and dusty before her,
the sun beating down hotly.   She had not gone
far when she turned, startled at hearing herself
greeted by name in the familiar Quaker tongue.
Her gaze rested upon a tall, corpulent man,
whom she recognized as a secret agent of
Lord Howe's.   He belonged to a society of
Friends, who, while loyal to the king, were passive as far as any public observation might de-

termine. Through General Stirling she had
learned of this man's position, he being stationed
at one of the city entrances to point out obnox-
ious persons coming in from the country.
Having from the first an instinctive dislike of
him, she acknowledged his greeting coldly and
continued her way.

"Didst thou come alone, friend?" asked the
Quaker, falling into step at her side. His
unctious voice grated on her.

"You have eyes," she answered shortly.
She remembered passing the entrance where
he was stationed several times when she had
been riding in the country with Armand. Invariably had the lad drawn his horse up to the
man's side, engaging in a little chat with him
while she had waited, taking no heed of the conversation, although indulgent of her brother's
fancy.

The Quaker kept beside her. Both were
silent.

Suddenly Mademoiselle de Berny, grown
suspicious and irritated at the man's insistence,
turned and faced him. "Monsieur," she said,
standing still, "what is it you desire of me?"
Recalling the miller's statement that her brother
had been met by a Quaker, her suspicion found
vent before he could reply. "Where is my
brother? You were seen with him yesterday."

"Hast thou missed him?" he asked urbanely.

"You know well I have," she retorted hotly.

"Where should I have seen thy brother?"
he asked.

His large and flabby face with its infantile
pinkness of skin was unchangeably bland. As
she met the cunning gaze of his small eyes, the
white lashes blinking continuously behind the
clumsy spectacles he wore, her dislike flamed
into anger.

"You wretched Quaker!" she cried; "you
wretched hypocrite! If you know where my
brother is, and refuse to tell me, I swear you
shall be whipped out of town, if not strung up
by the thumbs!"

He gave her a malevolent gaze but remained
silent.

She pointed down the road back of her.
"Go," she cried, "go, lest you repent it when
I return to Philadelphia. But, hark ye, Monsieur, and you have lied to me, your back shall
smart for it."

She moved on swiftly. When she had gone
some distance she glanced back and saw that he
was standing still watching her. She turned
and went on, fighting a nervous fear which
threatened to take possession of her. At last
where the road made a slight curve she seated
herself on the trunk of a fallen tree and waited.
But a little while had elapsed ere she saw from
her concealed position the Quaker peering down
the road, the light glancing on his spectacles as
he came stealthily towards her. A few moments

ago her heart had beaten hard with fear. But as the danger one flees is greater than when one turns and faces it, so now her fright faded. And so like some great gray cat creeping timorously did the fellow seem, that she was seized with a desire well-nigh irresistible to laugh.

"Many a true word is spoken in jest," she murmured, shaking her pretty head in keen amusement; "but little did I think, Rachel Mott, when I sent you word by the miller that I was fallen into the clutches of the Evil One, that he should prove of your sect and wear your colors!"

She allowed the Quaker to pass a little way by her before she made known her presence.

"Methinks you mistook me, Friend Broadbrim," she called after him cheerily; "did I not say the other direction?" illustrating her sentence by an airy wave of her hand.

She sat laughing at his discomfiture while he strove to maintain his habitual meekness of expression. Where he stood the sides of the road diverged widely, and in the centre of the broad space thus made stood an ancient and gnarled apple tree with low spreading branches. It was late in blossoming, and showed but scant promise of fruit in its tight red buds, as if its sap partook of the quality of the frozen and reluctant blood of old age. One branch stretched out across the road like a menacing arm, held over the Quaker and the young girl.

Some curious fancy communicated itself to Mademoiselle de Berny, and she moved along the log on which she was seated, out from the shade into the sunlight.

"Monsieur," she said, pointing upwards, "that branch hangs like a gallows limb above you."

He shook his forefinger menacingly at her. "The Lord rebuketh them who suspect others of evil. I, beholding thee alone, on a road frequented by ungodly men, did feel that the Lord appointed me a shepherd for one of his lambs and so did follow thee, receiving thy ill-will with meekness, for is it not bidden us that if we are smitten on one cheek to turn the other?"

"There are wolves as well as shepherds to be met with," she said; "and the silly lamb must look well else he might be deceived by the wolf in sheep's clothing—"

"Snares and pitfalls are before the feet of the ungodly," he interrupted.

"'Twere right good wisdom then that you save your soul and follow not in my path," she retorted. "I warned you once, Monsieur. Now you had better turn and go, unless you can tell me aught of my brother."

"'Twas but for a short while that I saw him," he admitted sullenly.

"Oh," she cried eagerly with an imploring gesture, "you saw him?"

"Yea, he was on his way to the rebels' camp, whither he had a friend he told me," answered the Quaker.

"Did he reach there?" she asked.

"Nay, I cannot answer thy every question. Can I tell thee how every blade of grass bends," he answered, "how should I know thy brother's every step, whether he falleth into the river or reacheth the rebels safely?"

"Monsieur," said the girl sternly, "I like not your manner. It savors of an impertinence for which I have no liking. Be careful lest you vex me too far, and your thumbs get stretched for it. Have you aught to eat with you?"

Sullenly he drew from his pocket some bread and cheese and laid it in her lap.

"I would not be of too great fastidiousness," she said, undoing the paper in which the food was wrapped, and turning the bread over lightly with one finger; "yet, by my faith, Friend Broadbrim, my conscience is more dainty than my stomach and cannot digest this unblest bread. Yet will I say grace before meat."

"Thou idolatrous Papist woman," cried the Quaker, recoiling as she made the sign of the cross.

Mademoiselle de Berny, beginning to eat the bread and cheese with relish, paused to laugh merrily as he turned and walked back in the

direction from which he had come. "Hasten,"
she called, "hasten, good friend Broadbrim,
meek servant of the Lord, hasten as if the
devil were at thy heels!"

He paused a moment and looked back, seeing her not only as she appeared then, but with
a vision in his mind of her disdainful airs in
Philadelphia. He recalled the crimson cloak
she had been in the habit of wearing, and which
whenever he had seen it was like unto a banner
of the Romish church flaunting in the Quaker
city. He shook his finger at her, his hand
trembling in his wrath.

"Yea, so would I quicken my steps, thou
idle Papist Frenchwoman," he spoke sourly,
"for doth not the Good Book bid us flee the
Scarlet Woman?"

Mademoiselle de Berny finished her lunch-
eon, putting what remained of the bread in
her pocket in case of further need. Her
countenance still showed traces of her sobbing
in the forest, but her nature, spontaneously
hopeful and happy, reasserted itself in strong
reaction of past grief.

For several miles she pressed on resolutely.
But the Quaker's words had left their sting in
her heart, and at last she no longer felt confident that Armand had reached Valley Forge
safely. Her anxiety returned, increased ten-
fold. Where she passed a thick copse, she
would stop, and parting the branches look

fearfully in, her intense nervousness filling her
with dread lest she should see his dead body.
Often pausing, she would call his name over
and over again. But in reply there was but
the echo of her anguished voice. Utterly exhausted at last, she seated herself on the
ground beneath a tree at some distance off
the road. She rested her head against the
trunk, her eyes closing wearily. The murmur of the river sounded dreamily near. Now,
it was Armand's voice, his dear voice beseeching her not to be troubled. Her tired frame
relaxed, her lids quivering slightly. She drew
a long, sighing breath, her head drooping on
her breast. She was asleep. Had the party
of Queen's Rangers, headed by General Stirling and the officer she had encountered that
morning, but glanced aside at that particular
point as they galloped down the road, they
would have discovered the object of their
search. But they passed, and returned within
an hour, unconscious as she of their nearness.

It was well on in the afternoon when Mademoiselle de Berny awakened, startled as she
glanced at the sun which hung low in the west
to see how long she had slept. She arose
dazedly in her half-roused consciousness, leaning against the tree with one hand, her brows
drawn together frowningly, as she strove to
collect her faculties. As she stood thus, a
party of light horse swung around a turn of

the road — a flash of blue amidst a cloud of
dust.   From her position she but caught
a glimpse of them, and she hastened forward
to intercept the riders, reaching the road at a
point but slightly in advance of the horsemen,
whose uniforms of buff and blue proved them
to be of the Continental Army.   The officer,
a young fellow of about twenty, drew up his
horse to inquire of the young girl if she had
passed a party of British cavalry, who had
been reported to have approached the American line that afternoon.   His accent, although
he spoke in English, proclaimed him a Frenchman.   In removing his cocked hat to address
her, he revealed a high receding forehead, from
which the red hair was brushed back and
braided in a long queue, looped up, and tied
with a ribbon.   His sharp, bright face, attrac-
tive despite its insignificant features and protruding hazel eyes, no less than his French
accent in her ears, homesick for the sound of
her native language, inspired confidence.   In
another moment she was relating rapidly to him
in French, with many excitable gestures, her
brother's disappearance, her subsequent following him, that the British seen had doubtless
been a searching party for her.   To her great
relief she learned that her brother had reached
the American encampment safely in the afternoon of the preceding day.

  " We will take you to him," said the officer.

He dismounted, standing a moment and looking with evident hesitation down the road. "I doubt if it be worth while to follow those fellows further," he said, turning. "If you, Mademoiselle," smiling, "were the object of that expedition which ended in failure, my heart stirs to something of sympathy for my foe." He ordered one of his men to dismount, remove his horse's saddle, and strap on a folded blanket in its stead. He then assisted her to mount. The soldier swung himself on a comrade's horse back of the rider, seated sideways as a woman and carrying the discarded saddle. The road following the river wound through so dense a forest that they seemed to be riding in a green twilight. So low hung the branches that they bowed their heads continually.

Mademoiselle de Berny's face regained color and brightness, as a flower after rain, albeit she was so wearied she could scarcely keep her seat on the horse. She and the young officer rode abreast in front of the men. The two chatted gayly in their native language. The young man's personality expressed the intense organism and energy accorded the possessor of like fiery hue of hair. For love of liberty, he told his companion, he left his bride, the gayety of the court; ay, incurred the displeasure of Louis, to go to America there to enter the Continental Army as a volunteer, although he had since been honored by pro-

motion to the rank of Major General. He was
the Marquis de La Fayette. And the name of
Mademoiselle? De Berny? Ah, yes, he had
acquaintance with her uncle the Abbé de Berny.
He remembered that he had been one of the
few to side with His Majesty, and to protest against the recognition of America's need.
"But we are younger, Mademoiselle," continued the young man; "your uncle belonging to the old school of our nobility cannot
change easily those ideas in which he has been
born and bred. Yet, thank God, the younger
blood has triumphed, and doubtless my news
that Louis has at last acknowledged the independence of the colonies is old to your ears.
'Twas less than a month ago that the winds
of heaven bore *La Sensible* to Falmouth har-
bor, and a herald from our fair country stepped
upon the land to proclaim the alliance."

"An imposing alliance," said Mademoiselle
de Berny, "making France's policy an inter-
national jest! Louis signing a treaty with a
handful of a brother-monarch's subjects in
insurrection!"

"This is no insurrection, Mademoiselle,"
answered her companion with deep gravity,
"but a revolution, the sound of whose cannon
will reverberate in all Europe, where arbitrary
power weighs heavily on the people. The
liberty for which we are fighting inspires me
with an ardent enthusiasm. Ah, you smile,

Mademoiselle! Are you unfriendly to the
Colonies? And you a Frenchwoman?" he
added in deep and visibly hurt reproach.
"Where is your love of liberty?"

She shrugged her shoulders daintily, laughing. "I am not a man," she said airily; "can
I go to war? Why should I concern myself
with these quarrelling English? Because a
handful of Americans are in rebellion against
their king, should I concern myself, or weep,
perforce, that I, a woman, may not go to war?"

"I know one woman," he responded with a
marked sternness, seeming strange to his youth
and gentle manner, "who is, perhaps, even
younger than you. But her love of liberty
made her give her husband to this revolution,
putting in jeopardy that life dearer to her than
her own. Ah, but women do go to war! In
their husbands' and lovers' hearts the thought
of them abides as one with freedom. She of
whom I speak is a Frenchwoman. Were she
to hear you, her sister, express such sentiment
her cheek would redden with shame."

His companion made no reply. Silently
they rode along. La Fayette's eyes saw not
the clayey road, but instead the soft green
fields of sunny France, the vineyards sloping
to the river, the orchard blowing sweet in
blossom, the old gray wall of a château against
the blue sky. And she was there in that beloved country, her constant thought a prayer

for him.   Could the young wife whose own
fair hands had buckled on his sword, bidding
his courage prove worthy of her love, have
seen him at that moment, doubtless he would
have appeared to her more a homesick boy
than a young General honored for his valor.

The party halted at the King of Prussia Tavern, an inn famous for its good cheer.   Its sign
emblazoned by the figure of a warrior on horseback, painted by Gilbert Stuart, hung creaking
in the breeze.

" Mademoiselle," said La Fayette, his sensitive face once more serene, " I can permit you
to go no further without partaking of some re-
freshment."   He lifted her from the horse and
accompanied her inside.

The inn was typical of those of the period.
Along the front ran a verandah.   At one end
was a bench with shining basins and homespun
towels hanging above on the lattice-work to dry,
for when a traveller arose in the morning he
washed his face not in his room but on the
piazza.   At La Fayette's command, the innkeeper, an old pipe-smoking German, carried
ale to the soldiers waiting outside.

" We have none such quaint inns in France,
Marquis," smiled the young girl, noting the
sanded floor, the great tub of water wherein
melons and cucumbers, pitchers of milk and
bottles of wine were set to cool.   A rosy coun-
try-maid, returning from the spring, paused to

jest with the soldiers. One stalwart fellow, he who had resigned his horse to Mademoiselle de Berny's service, leant over to drink from the pitcher held up by a pair of round arms, wet and glowing from the spring water. In his haste to snatch a kiss after drinking, the soldier tipped the pitcher over, to his own confusion and the guffaws of his comrades, while the drenched damsel made her way once more to the spring.

Mademoiselle de Berny, sipping a cup of coffee, laughed as she witnessed the scene through the open door. The soldiers were a hardy set of men, unshaven and shabbily clothed. With the exception of the Marquis de La Fayette, she noticed that none of the party possessed complete uniforms.

"Womanlike you are criticising our dress, Mademoiselle," said her companion, divining her thought. "True, we are in a luckless plight. 'Tis a joke amongst the officers that when one is invited to dine at headquarters, he must borrow his uniform — a hat from this man, a coat and a clean shirt from that, a decent pair of boots from another. But yesterday an officer appeared *au grande parole*, attired in a blanket, like an Indian chief," he added, laughing heartily and with a boyish infectiousness. "But let us hasten, if you have finished. I fear a storm is rising."

The sun was setting, dimly obscured by an

ominous vapor through which it shone like a
ball of fire. Heavy clouds were forming slowly
at the horizon, casting great purple shadows on
the green meadows. Not a leaf moved. The
songs of birds were hushed. In one corner of
a field some cattle had drawn closely together,
standing with lowered heads. The men also
became silent, as sharing the oppression of
nature before a storm.

Mademoiselle de Berny and General La Fayette exchanged no words, each absorbed in
thought.

In the young girl's eyes was an expression
at once shy and defiant, as if she would fain
have turned and gone the other way despite
her desire to see her brother.

Chapter V

DESCENDING a long, steep hill they came suddenly upon Valley Forge. Never had Mademoiselle de Berny looked upon so desolate a scene. With the fading of day, a raw and chilly breeze sprang up. It rose cold and damp from the river and blew sharp in their faces — a cheerless greeting. Between them and the encampment the Schuylkill flowed, gray and turbulent, beneath the rising storm. In the angle formed by it and a little creek emptying into it from the north lay a village, consisting of row upon row of log huts. A small stone house near the creek was pointed out to Mademoiselle by the Marquis de La Fayette as the headquarters of the army. Beyond the encampment, far as the eye could reach, stretched a great barren plain, sloping to a far hill-line. The ford, which was very wide, was difficult in passing, the river running so high that the water was well above the horses' knees. In the swift current on the unsteady stones at the bottom, the animals' feet slipped constantly. La Fayette, guiding his own horse, held firmly with his other hand Mademoiselle de Berny's bridle. As the little party reached the other side, there was sounded the muffled yet shrill tones of the tattoo for evening prayer.

"The service will be short," said La Fayette, "and I think we will find it pleasanter to wait until it is over than to attempt to make our way through the ranks now. But let us move nearer."

Never in her bright life had the young girl imagined there existed such pale, desolate, and ragged men as soldiers issued from the huts, obeying the summons of the tattoo. The chaplain mounted the stump, a meagre, bowed figure in black, with thin white hair. Near him was stationed a body of officers. The entire army had an air of silent expectation. Suddenly her roving glance was attracted toward a man wrapped in a blue military cape advancing through the soldiers, who parted with profound reverence. The newcomer towered head and shoulders above the majority. As he drew nearer, walking swiftly, bearing himself with a dignity which possessed something of an austere grandeur, she saw his countenance plainly. He removed his hat as the chaplain gave the opening prayer, revealing a dome-like head, the light brown hair, heavily sprinkled with gray, tied with a black ribbon. The face was massively cut and of unusual pallor, the nose prominent, the mouth compressed, the underlip and chin slightly protruding. His glance dwelt momentarily on the young girl, but she felt he had not even observed her as she met the gaze of those shadowed eyes, which seemed to look inward rather than afar.

The chaplain, raising his hand, — the trembling and wrinkled hand of an old man, — announced the text: "They that take the sword shall perish by the sword."

As a bell, though cracked, tolls none the less surely for death, so the text uttered in the high, quavering voice of old age, shrill above the vague yet vast murmur of the crowd, seemed like an unalterable proclamation of fate. As the cracked bell, whose solemn message none might gainsay, so the feeble penetrating voice uttered divine justice: "An eye for an eye, a tooth for a tooth!" As one would be deaf to the death-knell, so with a like impulse did Mademoiselle de Berny look away shudderingly from the speaker. Vainly her glance swept the masses for her brother. Yet, regardless of her anxiety, she was half-fearful lest she should see Richard Heyward. But she saw no familiar face among these gaunt-bearded men, sunken cheeked and hollow eyed. On some of the ragged coats were pinned heart-shaped pieces of red flannel. These bits of cloth were worn on the left breast. This novel detail of the scene excited Mademoiselle de Berny's curiosity, so that she whispered to her companion. He answered in a low tone — for the service still continued

— that it was a decoration conferred by General Washington on those soldiers who distinguished themselves by bravery, privileging the wearer to pass the camp guards as if he were a commissioned officer.

"Ah, Mademoiselle," said the young Frenchman sadly, "there is a pathos in the simple decoration which rends my heart, so humble are the favors His Excellency can bestow. With what repressed emotion have I seen him pin on these badges! His great and generous spirit is offended at the mean, poor token."

In the ranks nearest to the little party stood a man whose tattered clothing failed to detract from the dignity of his magnificent physique. Suddenly he turned and Mademoiselle de Berny saw the red badge on his breast. But no intelligence was in his face, and she saw that he was quite mad. Fascinated she stared long at him, unmindful of the wild and mournful gaze he in his turn bestowed upon her, until at last she became conscious of it, and looked away. This was what war meant, this — to suffer, to bear nakedness, hunger, and cold, to leave wife and child, to go mad, perhaps, beneath the strain — wearing as insignia for valor no jewelled cross nor glittering star, but a rude and ragged piece of cloth indicative of the wearer's bravery, and the poverty of that country for which he fought. All thought of self, even her desire to see her brother, faded as the mournfulness of the scene was impressed upon her bright nature. On her were cast the frequent glances of men, little accustomed to the sight of a young and beautiful woman. One last shaft of light from the departing day pierced the heavy clouds, and fell upon her singling out her figure in the multitude, and lighting up her appalled and wondering face from which the hood of her cloak had fallen back.

At the conclusion of the service, the officer whom she had noticed came forward and greeted her kindly. It was His Excellency, General Washington. He listened attentively to her explanation of her appearance at Valley Forge.

"It will not be possible, considering certain movements now on foot, for me to return you and your brother at once to Philadelphia," he said, "without exposing somewhat of my own plans and with probable inconvenience, even danger to you both on the road. But within a few days I am confident I shall be able to do so." In his expression appeared a gleam of that quiet humor, which seldom seen in his face was never forgotten by those who once observed it. "My child," he continued, "any papers found upon your brother's person were delivered to me, and great was my amazement to find that the letter your brother so anxiously desired to return to Major Heyward

proved no treasonable communication, but
seemed rather to investigate a field of which I
am ignorant, and which is presided over by a
much smaller but world-powerful general, who
conquers all hearts.   My child," he added
smilingly and removing his hat with a profound
bow, " I beg your pardon inasmuch as I read
a letter intended for your eyes only, and thinking that it would reach you most safely through
the writer, to him did I return your rightful
property."

But Mademoiselle de Berny made no reply.
The silken lashes of her down-cast eyes lay
upon her burning cheeks.   When at last she
looked up His Excellency had departed, and
she caught a glimpse of his tall figure moving
rapidly through the ranks.   She and the
Marquis de La Fayette and his orderly were
isolated figures.   The cavalry which had accompanied the young Frenchman on the afternoon's expedition had been dismissed by him,
and he now but waited until the troops should
have dispersed for supper before escorting his
fair country-woman to headquarters, where she
would be welcomed by the wife of His Excellency, who was then in camp.

"Monsieur," said the young girl, " I have
looked in all directions for my brother, but I
fail to see him."

But as she spoke she saw him emerge from
a group of soldiers some distance away.   He

walked slowly in her direction, which was
opposite to that in which the encampment lay.
She would have spurred her horse to go to
meet him, or have dismounted and hastened
forward on foot, had not some intangible and
jarring impression made by his strange environment communicated itself to her so that the
warmth rising in her at their prospective greeting was suddenly chilled, and the eager words
died on her lips as she sat motionless watching
him approach her.   At his side was the crazed
soldier she had observed some moments since,
and who had disappeared after a while from her
view.   Beside his stalwart figure, Armand with
his slenderness and length of limb had a fawn-
like grace.   The lad sauntered easily at his
companion's side, one hand resting on the hilt
of his father's sword, the other on the head
of the Great Dane.   His fair head was un-
covered and turned toward the soldier with
whom he was talking.   The impression which
the first glimpse of her brother had given
Mademoiselle de Berny had caused her to feel
what seemed merely a physical chill, but now
as he drew nearer with his strange companion,
who nodded constantly with a foolish smile to
what was said, she put her hands against her
breast as if the cold had struck down to her
heart.   Even La Fayette was unconsciously
made silent, and awaited developments curiously.   The long grass at the feet of the three,

the boy and soldier and hound walking abreast,
rippled like green waves in the breeze.   Where
were they going at this hour, with a storm rising?   Surely the boy, blind though he was,
knew where the encampment lay by the voices
of the men, the brisk stir and bustle of sound
as they prepared supper.   The huts were
shrouded in gloom.   But here and there newly
made fires leaped up redly.   Only on the
green meadow sloping to the river the light of
day still lingered, and brought out the three
figures with a soft brilliancy.   Behind and
above the huts the sky was black, but in the
east still remained a patch of blue.   Suddenly
Armand flung back his head and laughed; the
sweet tones of his mirth reverberated faintly.
He thrust his arm through his companion's in
close comradeship.

   "Monsieur," cried Mademoiselle de Berny
sharply to La Fayette, "that man is mad! He
is mad, and do you see — my brother does not
know it!"

   Recognizing her voice, the Great Dane raised
its head barking excitedly.   It bounded to her
side, leaped upon her, lapping her hands, then
left her and ran back to his master, then again
to her.   The boy put out his hands grop-
ingly.   "What is it?" he kept repeating.   He
stood still turning his head from side to side
and with extended hands.   As if some spell
enjoining silence had been broken Mademoi-

selle de Berny called to him.   Her companion,
divining her desire to go to him, dismounted
and assisted her to the ground, flinging the
reins to his orderly.

"See, Mademoiselle," he said, keeping at
her side, "your brother knew your voice.   He
calls you."

But she, breaking into a little run in her
haste, did not reply.   Another moment and
her arms were around her brother and she was
sobbing and laughing and uttering soft inarticulate sounds of endearment.   "Armand," she
said at last, "why did you go without telling
me?"

"Because I wished to," he answered crossly,
striving to release himself from her embrace.

As she looked at him in astonishment, she
saw there were tears of vexation in his eyes.

"Why did you come after me?" he said;
"I am no baby.   I can take care of myself.
I will not be put in leading-strings.   Look,
what will these soldiers think to see me with a
woman at my heels, as a child with its nurse?"
He made a desperate, impassionated gesture
and burst into enraged weeping.   "I will not
have you forever watching and following me,
Diane.   My father did as he pleased, and I
will do so, too, or I will kill myself! I will kill
myself!"

Mademoiselle de Berny's and La Fayette's
gaze met in sympathy.   In the mind of each

was the same thought as the angry sobbing of
the lad smote their ears. Alas, that he should
be so defiant, who was indeed so very helpless;
who rebelled at protection against the world, at
whose mercy he would be were none to guard
him; who sought to command whereas he was
fated to inspire but pity!

"Armand," said his sister very gently as she
comprehended his wounded pride, his vexation
and mortification, "I am sorry. I will do
whatever you wish, dear, and I will never follow you again if it vexes you. Shall I leave
you and return to Philadelphia?"

He raised his head then, his face clearing and showing some gratification but more
obstinacy.

"Yes, you must go back, Diane," he said
importantly. "Then when I return —"

The Marquis de La Fayette interrupted him
with some impatience, "Monsieur," he said,
"Mademoiselle, your sister, has been refused
permission by His Excellency to leave Valley
Forge for several days, owing to certain prospective movements."

"Very well," said the boy easily. He was
entirely pacified by his sister's gentleness.
"But you must not tell any one that you
came after me, Diane."

He shook off the hand of the insane soldier
who had drawn near and touched his shoulder,
seeking to attract his attention. "Go home,

fellow," he said, pointing toward the encampment, "go home at once." The man comprehended the words and gesture and moved off
quickly.

Great drops of rain were falling. Hurriedly
the young Frenchman assisted Mademoiselle
de Berny upon her horse and mounted his own
steed. Young Stirling swung himself up behind La Fayette. The three reached headquarters just as the storm commenced in good
earnest. It proved one of those violent and
electrical tempests which occur in the spring of
the year.

But within the log cabin which General
Washington, owing to the smallness of the
house, had had built for a dining-room and
which adjoined the main building, there was
light and warmth, although in one corner of
the ceiling the rain forced an ingress and dripped
continuously. It was an oblong room with
lowering rafters, the cracks in the log walls
plastered with clay. Candles shone at intervals
down the table, which was of such length as to
necessitate being placed diagonally across the
floor. A fire burned merrily on the hearth,
casting grotesque shadows and reflecting redly
upon those seated near by. In the wavering
light the grim poverty of the room was strik-
ingly manifested, and the faces surrounding the
board acquired a mysterious mellowness as the
faces of an old painting.

The food was meagre, the two tin dishes of greens being supplemented by a hot and substantial pie of wild pigeons, flocks of which passed over the encampment in vast numbers, flying so near the ground as to be killed with clubs and poles.   Massive silver goblets, such as were used by the Marshals of France, reflected the gleaming of the candles.   Seated next to Mademoiselle de Berny was her brother, with whom since their meeting she had had no further opportunity to converse.   From time to time her gaze rested anxiously upon him. His soft hair was ill cared for, his ruffled shirt was limp and spattered with mud.   Between their chairs crouched the Great Dane.   Now and then the lad fed the dog a bit of food, but she noted that he himself ate little.

At the head of the table His Excellency's wife, a portly, middle-aged woman, attired in a russet gown with cap and kerchief of white muslin, exercised a motherly supervision over this military family.   Beside her plate lay a half-knit sock and a ball of gray yarn.   Of one officer she made inquiry regarding the price of eggs and butter.

Mademoiselle de Berny, glancing at her timepiece bearing on its back a miniature of Marie Antoinette, smiled.   So this was Lady Washington — this good, unpretentious countrywoman.   Ah, had not she seen at the Little Trianon a queen enact the rôle of country-

woman, a royal dairy maid, a coquetry with labor !
She recalled the charming and artificial garden
with its conventional designs, its flower-bordered walks, the tiny lake with its swans. She
saw again L'Austrichine with her bright blue
eyes, her powdered hair dressed with plumes,
with patches of black plaster to emphasize the
fairness of her skin. The sparkling necklace
around the slim neck seemed to detach the
queenly head from the undignified figure in
shepherdess costume with a milking-stool under
one arm and with bits of butter and flour clinging to the royal fingers. Ah, the glamour of
those days when a shepherd's crook was a
sceptre, when a gay court betook itself to the
country to churn butter as a jest, to skim milk
as a diversion, to drive the cows to pasture as
the cream of pleasure ! She turned as her
neighbor, an elderly officer, Baron Von Steuben,
on whose broad breast glittered innumerable
medals won in the Prussian Army, addressed
her, deploring her lack of appetite and urging
another dish upon her. He had been devoting
himself to her with unceasing attention, putting
upon her plate the choicest bits of pigeon.

" I fear my plates which were once of tin,
Mademoiselle de Berny," said General Washington, joining in the conversation, " are now
but little better than rusty iron, rather too
much worn for delicate stomachs ; still they
may yet serve in the busy and active move-

G

ments of the campaign. To-morrow, I promise
you, you shall be served by something better
than this present fare. I have some droves of
fat cattle coming from New England which
should have been here to-day, but probably —"

"I fear your fat cattle will make high living
for your enemy, your Excellency," interrupted
his guest. "I was near to being trampled
upon by them this morning, as they were driven
by the Queen's Rangers along the road to
Philadelphia."

Washington uttered a bitter exclamation.
"Did you see more than one drove, Mademoiselle?" he asked.

"But one," she said; "perhaps fifty or one
hundred head."

His face cleared. "There is still a chance
of saving the rest. I shall send a detachment
at once to guard the road. Near Frankfort,
you said?" He gave an order to his secretary, and the officer rose and left the room.

"You must needs send a goodly number,"
said Mademoiselle de Berny, remembering the
shabby Continental troops. "The British are
stout fellows, well uniformed and armed —"

"Ah, my child," interrupted Washington,
laughing, "but your British don't fight! The
ragged fellows are the boys for fighting!"

"Eh, Mam'selle," said Baron Von Steuben,
wagging his jovial head confidentially, "dey
fight, dese Americaines, for de love of de lib-

erty; but mein Gott, vot discipline! I vork in de field, but ils ne comprendent pas. Den vot say I, mon ami Walker," he asked, turning to his interpreter, a young and handsome man, whose glances in Mademoiselle de Berny's direction had been frequent. "I vill tell you vot I call," continued the Baron, "I halt my horse, I wave my hand. Viens, mon ami Walker, I call, viens mon bon ami. Sacrebleu Gott, verdame de gaucherie of dese badants! Je ne pius plus! I can curse dem no more!"

Amidst the general laughter and conversation following, the dishes and cloth were removed from the table, with the exception of the silver goblets. These were filled with Madeira wine by Washington's body servant, an old white-haired negro. Plates of hickory nuts and apples were passed down the board. Lady Washington shook her head in refusal of the dessert. Her good and tireless hands were busy knitting. She took little part in the conversation, listening with a placid smile to the sallies of the officers. His Excellency was also silent in general, speaking when he did so, in a low, almost constrained tone, but listening with kindly attention when addressed. His enormous hands, whose long and bony fingers bespoke that love of detail so strongly manifested in his actions, separated the empty shells from those containing the kernels, into two exact little piles. The other women, following Lady Washington's example, were knitting. The young and beautiful wife of Alexander Hamilton, Washington's secretary, had placed a skein of the coarse yarn on Baron Von Steuben's hands, and had drawn her chair some distance back, that she might wind the ball more readily. Mademoiselle de Berny, her hand resting on her brother's shoulder, was a stranger to the rude and simple festivity. Her mouth quivered with subtle scorn. Richard Heyward's position appeared in a better, if in a meaner and poorer, light as well. Surely, she thought, her alien glance noting the meagre room and shabby fare, his actions must have ensued from some mistaken principle, and not from any glory he might win allied to such poverty. Where was the pomp and ceremony of war? And his reward? She looked at Lady Washington. Doubtless this kind and domestic woman presented him at times with those labors of her hands, on which she was so busily engaged at present. As she turned her eyes away she met those of the Marquis de La Fayette. He, guessing the tenor of her thought, felt the blood rush to his face. Then a very young and impulsive man, possessing an ardent love for his own country as well as for the new republic he espoused, he was intensely mortified by the attitude he intuitively felt was taken by his country-woman. To his impetuous nature this

attitude on her part was as an insult from one
of his own blood to the General he worshipped
and to whom he was as a son, and of whose
hospitality both Mademoiselle de Berny and
himself were then in acceptance.

But her amusement deepened as she on her
part read aright the fiery glance of her awkward and red-haired young countryman, whose
high-flown virtue carried him to ridiculous extremes. And a corresponding flash of opposition came into her expression, as he arose
and proposed her health not only as an honored guest at Valley Forge, but as a representative of France, the alliance of which with
the United States had been so recently made.

Young Stirling's voice rang out sharply.
" My father was killed in the King's Army."
He pushed his goblet away, the liquid splash-
ing over.

There was a momentary silence. Then
Baron Von Steuben, whose interpreter had repeated the remark to him, roared with laughter,
his fat sides shaking with merriment at the
lad's spirit.

" How falls it that this young girl is your
sister?" inquired General Washington.

"She is my half-sister, your Excellency," answered young Stirling, turning his sightless
gaze upon the speaker. On either cheek
burned a spot of color.

The helpless, sensitive face touched his questioner's great heart. "Then your sister only claims our courtesy as hailing from France," he said; "you, young sir, we must account a prisoner-of-war."

"Yes," said the boy, nodding importantly, his face illumined by pride, "yes, your Excellency, a prisoner-of-war."

"There are still those of my nation, among whom I am one, your Excellency," said Mademoiselle de Berny, with a quick, defiant glance at La Fayette, "who remember that these insurgents who accept our aid to-day stood with their present enemy twenty years ago against the French regiments in America. And the leader of those Provincials, General Washington?"

A gleam of fire lighted Washington's cold countenance. "You are a nation of good fighters, Mademoiselle." He turned to his wife. "I was a young man then, my dear Patsy," he said, "a young man with warmer blood than I have to-day." A rare smile was on his face as his glance once more rested on the young girl — the indulgent smile maturity accords its vanished youth. On memory's wall a picture kept its grace somehow, — the bud of beauty which had borne no fruit, — the unrequited love of his youth. Had he not in his disappointment and passion expressed his sorrow in a poem?

> Oh, ye Gods, why should my poor resistless heart
> Stand to oppose thy might and power,

At last surrender to Cupid's feathered dart,
And now lays bleeding every hour,
For her that's pitiless of my griefs and woes
And will not on me pity take ?

Truly, he thought, smiling, Providence had in all prudence taken the pen from his hand and given in place a sword.

"Youth is very distant, my dear Patsy," he said, sighing; "further than any stretch of years, Mademoiselle," he added, turning to his guest, "join us at least in pledging an honored foe which has become a friend. You, a daughter of France, we cannot esteem an enemy."

The Marquis de La Fayette lifted high his silver goblet. "To France," he cried, his face aglow, his eyes dwelling on his fair country-woman. "To France we will drink, Mademoiselle, that our country may by the grace of God enjoy all liberty which is compatible with our monarchy, our position, and our customs."

The nobility in Mademoiselle de Berny's character responded to the generous and kindly spirit of the little company. Her face softened, her eyes were full of a shamed yet half-defiant pride as her slender fingers tightened around the stem of the goblet.

"Ah, Messieurs," she protested, "you force me to become your friend."

Amidst the sturdy applause and laughter, she and the young Marquis touched their glasses to the toast.

Chapter VI

THE heavy storm which had arisen that evening died down toward nine o'clock into a slight but stinging rain, blown by a strong wind. At a rude pine table in one of the log huts of the encampment a young man sat writing by the light of a fire blazing on the hearth. With the exception of the table and the chair, there was no other furniture save two beds opposite each other, made of straw on boards and covered by blankets. In the clay, plastering the cracks in the log walls, were driven several pegs ; on one hung an army cape, the scarlet lining of which showed where one corner had been tossed back. On another peg was a cocked hat, the light glinting on the gold cord around its crown. The wind blew open the door made of split oak slabs. The gust of air whirled the sheets of paper off the table in a mad skurry around the room. With an impatient exclamation the lonely inmate rose, and shoved the door to with his foot. The sullen sound of the storm vexed him, and he felt unstrung and nervous as he collected the scattered papers. He rescued a piece from the fire. As he blew out the flame of one burning cor-

ner, he saw the door again pushed open, this
time slowly, as by one whose hands were weak
against the heavy oak. A second more and
the Great Dane entered, tugging at his chain,
almost dragging his slender master in. The
boy was wet with rain, his face glowing from
buffeting with the storm.

"Here is Diane," he said, leaning against
the door to hold it open.

Mademoiselle de Berny, well-nigh blown in,
blinded by the sudden light and the loosened
tresses of her hair flying across her eyes, did
not at first recognize the owner of the hut
which she entered. When she did so, she
retreated to the door.

"You did not tell me you were staying with
Monsieur Heyward, Armand," she said, and
her voice rang sharply.

Baron Von Steuben, who with his interpreter had accompanied the young girl at her
request to see her brother's lodgings, followed
young Stirling and the hound over to the fire.
He held his hands to the blaze, the steam soon
rising from his wet garments. He spoke to
Mademoiselle de Berny, advising her to draw
nearer the fire.

But she ignored his solicitous regard. "You
did not tell me, Armand," she repeated
stormily.

"In a second, Diane," he called, kneeling at
his dog's side and unfastening the chain at-

tached to its collar. "Be still, you clumsy rascal!" He attempted to strike the dog, but slipped and fell on his side. "What was it you said, Diane?" he laughed, as the huge animal stood over him, its paws on his breast. He made a sudden grab at the hound's neck, and the two rolled over and over on the floor.

"Will you not go nearer the fire?" asked Heyward, addressing Mademoiselle de Berny. His face was pale, and he was visibly embarrassed. But she, struggling to control a corresponding embarrassment in herself, neither replied to nor looked at him, keeping her gaze fixed stormily on her brother as he wrestled with his dog. The rain glistened on the fine curls which had escaped from beneath her hood. Her hands held her cloak together with a nervous tightness. Both she and her host were instinctively conscious of an effort on the part of each other to carry off conventionally, in appearance at least, a position so delicate and at such a tension as to bear not the slightest touch. The unfortunate misunderstanding which had arisen during the period of courtship, and before any confession of their mutual love had been made, left them stranded, hopeless to meet each other with the frankness of friendship, and lacking the assurance of acknowledged lovers.

Lieutenant Walker, holding his hat, and leaning against the low wall, he himself so tall that his blond head nearly touched the ceiling, was looking admiringly at the young girl. " Mademoiselle de Berny is a veritable water-witch, Heyward," he said ; " her spirits rose high as the wind itself, till I thought she would fly away with it, and she must needs walk with her face set to the teeth of the gale. Yet I verily believe her cloak is not even damp."

" Ah, but it is," she said quickly, "and you, Monsieur, may hold it to dry, if you please."

The young man laughed and laid his hat on the table. Then he lifted the garment from her shoulders. So large was the cloak that he could hold up with ease but one portion at a time. He walked toward the fire, limping slightly from a wound in his left leg which had healed badly.

" See here, Baron Von Steuben," he said, "suppose you take a hand in this and lift the other side."

Heyward's sombre face lighted momentarily with amusement as he watched the two men blistering before the fire. Then he turned to Mademoiselle de Berny. She had drawn nearer the door. In the great square shadow flung by the cloak her face lost all color. Could he but have known it, her next sentence was the cry of her wounded heart to him. Her world had been suddenly turned around and the foundation on which she stood was proving unsure.

For Mademoiselle de Berny had come to Valley
Forge with perfect self-assurance, secure in her
conviction that as surely as she was in the right
so was Richard Heyward in the wrong, lacking
not only honor as a soldier, but gallantry as a
man in leaving her without an explanation.
But this last conclusion was altered by the fact
of his having written to her, although the letter
had miscarried, and, moreover, it needed merely
a glance at his troubled countenance to convince
her of his love, and that only the desperate need
of escaping arrest had made him leave Philadelphia as he did.   Now her vantage ground as
the accuser was swept from beneath her feet.
She, not looking at him, yet felt that in his
gaze was wonder at her appearance at Valley
Forge and some reproach that she had not
waited to hear from him.   Her heart sickened
with shame and humiliation as she saw herself
in the position of a woman seeking and not
contented to be sought.   The restless desire to
see him again, which had, to a certain extent,
actuated her in going in search of her brother
and which she had refused to admit, now forced
itself upon her, refusing longer to be ignored.
She forgot her brother.   Things were reduced
to one aspect.   She had followed Heyward to
the encampment.   She forced herself to look
at him and saw the perplexed surprise with which
he regarded her.   Her pale face crimsoned.
The brightness of her eyes was very near to tears.

"So you escaped, Monsieur," she said with ominous softness; "I perceive you are very wise. The quality you possess is, I have heard, the better part of valor. You have lived, shall I say, to fight another day?"

His face, sensitive and impassioned, quivered. She saw that he strove to answer, but the words choked him. She glanced at the other occupants of the hut. Her brother had flung himself on one of the low beds and lay with his arms around his dog and with the animal's paws around his neck. The two men now held the cloak up by the sleeves, and it looked like some dancing headless figure between them.

"You left Philadelphia unceremoniously," she continued; "but your fear as regarded me was unnecessary. I told you I should say naught. Yet 'twas doubtless natural that your opinion of my integrity should be colored by your knowledge of yourself."

"To my certain knowledge," he said coldly, turning so as to face her directly, "no one in Philadelphia knew of my position there except yourself. Still within a few hours after our conversation the British were made acquainted with the fact."

"Doubtless the walls had ears, Monsieur," she retorted icily.

He looked away. "I beg your pardon," he said dully; "it was only that — I could not understand how they procured information. I

did not really believe you had betrayed me.
I thought of our past friendship. It did not
seem possible. It was — I — men expect much
from women — not that they have the right,
but — "

"Women also have their ideals," she answered. She raised her voice to address Baron
Von Steuben in regard to her cloak.

"In von second, Mam'selle," he replied,
turning a red and perspiring face towards her,
" but von leettle second more and it vill be dry."

" But one little second more, Mademoiselle,"
echoed Lieutenant Walker, " and we shall melt
away. Your cloak will be no fit. I swear 'tis
warping with the heat ! "

Heyward laughed a mirthless laugh, in which
his nervousness, strung to a high tension, found
expression. Glancing at his companion, he became conscious of the fact that she had been
standing so near the half-open door that the
rain beat in upon her shoulders.

" Will you not go nearer the fire ? " he said
gently, " the hospitality I can offer you is poor,
but it is at your service." He reached behind
her and closed the door, shutting out the storm.

She moved slightly further into the interior
and leant against the wall. The extreme gentleness of his tone and manner, his harassed and
pained countenance, his total lack of comprehension that her bitter words were in reality
wrung from humiliation on her part, caused the

tears to rush to her eyes so that she closed
them, turning her head away against the wall.
Her nature, naturally generous, was outraged
by the ungenerous words to which she had given
utterance. Each taunt she had levelled at him
had rebounded to accentuate her pain. Humiliated though she was by the fact of her
having come to Valley Forge, that feeling was
slight compared to the mortification she now
experienced when he showed neither resentment nor anger, but pain and trouble at her
scorn. She moved nervously, her lips quivering. "I am so tired," she said with deepen-
ing shame at resorting to the plea of physical
weakness, knowing herself to be employing a
feminine subterfuge to maintain a lost ground
by reliance upon the gallantry of the masculine
nature. "I am so tired," she repeated, "I
would like to go to my room."

He saw she was white from exhaustion and
there were purple shadows under her eyes.
The vein along her cheek and temple, almost
imperceptible when she was well, now showed
plainly. He crossed the room to the fireplace.
"Let me have the cloak now, if you please,
Walker," he said; "Mademoiselle de Berny is
very tired, and the sooner she gets out of the
rain and cold the better it will be for her, I am
sure. Perhaps you will speak to Lady Washington and see that she has something hot to
drink," he added with anxiety.

The young lieutenant refused to relinquish the honor of himself wrapping the cloak around Mademoiselle. "'Tis as dry as a bone," he said, buttoning it for her and kneeling down to fasten the last buttons, secretly amused at the jealous glance of his host. "I swear I shall mix you the best toddy you ever tasted, Mademoiselle," he said, rising; "'tis out of the Baron's own flask," he laughed, "and mellow as the sunlight on a harvest day."

She smiled, striving not to yield to an almost overpowering weariness. She crossed the room to her brother, who sat on one of the rude beds stroking the hound's handsome head. "I am going, Armand," she said, bending to kiss him. "Sleep well, dear one," she murmured, "sleep well," lingering a moment with her face against his. He put his arm up around her neck drawing her closely to him.

"Good night," he said happily; "ah, Diane, is it not fine to be here? I'm so glad you came. It makes me laugh to think how surprised my father would be to know we were in the enemy's camp." He released her and bent his face to his dog's ear. "They'd better keep a sharp eye on us, Little Brother," he whispered gayly.

As Mademoiselle de Berny rose, her depression and lassitude were no longer apparent, held in subjection by her intense pride. She bade Heyward good night easily, as if he were some

chance acquaintance. He watched her as she
moved off with a light step, between General
Von Steuben and his secretary. Now the three
passed into shadow, then into alternate streams
of light from the partly open doors of the huts
on either side of the road. So she stepped
lightly into a future in which he had no part,
treading his love under foot as a thing un-
worthy. How had the right for which he had
sacrificed all turned against him, making him
appear base in her eyes. Jealously he watched
the tall figure of the young secretary, moving
with his characteristic limp closely by her side,
his head bent in talking to her.

Mademoiselle de Berny, glancing back, saw
him still standing in the doorway. She felt the
desolation of the solitary figure.

"Major Heyward," called young Stirling
petulantly, from his position on the bed, "I
am hungry. Can we not have some biscuit
and toddy?" He rose frowning. "I am so
hungry," he repeated crossly, "and I'm sick.
I don't feel well. Go, tell Diane I want her."

"Yes, my boy," answered Heyward absently,
turning from his position with a heavy sigh.
He closed the door and bolted it for the night.
"You shall have something in a moment," he
said kindly, striving to speak cheerily. He
stirred the fire briskly, and put on the kettle
of water. When it had boiled he filled two
pewter mugs with the toddy and put them with

H

some biscuits and a little fruit he had purchased
for his guest on the table.

"Draw up, Armand," he said cheerfully,
"and see if you will not feel better."

The boy ate hungrily, feeding his dog also
and allowing it to have some of the liquid
which the Great Dane swallowed with relish,
seated upright at its master's side, its intelligent
gaze observing his every motion. Heyward
neither ate nor drank anything, but sat with
one elbow on the table, his head resting on his
hand as he observed his companion. He was
alternately attracted and repelled by him. At
times he watched him hungrily, waiting until
young Stirling took some attitude in which his
own personality seemed lost, and he expressed
more his sister than himself. His laughter,
certain cadences of his voice, the turning of
his head, a gesture, recalled Mademoiselle de
Berny so vividly that there seemed revealed in
a sudden flash of light her own hidden self, as
if in some gay mood she had taken on the
masque of a boy. He had a curious dislike of
the fancy which mocked him by its lack of
reality, so that he felt hopeless and baffled as
one encountering conditions with which he is
powerless to deal. Armand, with the peculiar
sensitiveness of the blind, rose and went around
the table, standing by the young man's side.
He put out his hand. Heyward shivered
beneath the touch of those delicate fingers

which wandered over his face and hair. They were like ghostly touches of Mademoiselle's hands.

"Dear friend," said the lad pitifully, "what troubles you?"

The hound, catching the sad intonation of his master's voice, raised his head and howled mournfully.

Heyward laughed in grim amusement at this last expression of sympathy with his gloomy mood. "My dear little fellow," he said, catching the lad to him, "my dear boy, it's time for us to go to bed."

Mademoiselle de Berny had retired immediately to her room upon reaching headquarters. A colored woman brought her two lighted candles, and a cup of hot tea Lady Washington had prepared for her at the suggestion of Lieutenant Walker. On almost any other occasion the primitive simplicity of her room could not have failed to delight the young girl. But now her depression was so great that she scarcely observed her surroundings, taking no note of the white sanded floor, the high narrow bed pushed up primly in one corner, and draped with curtains of coarse linen, sweet and clean and smelling of lavender, the pewter bowl and pitcher on a shelf below a tiny cracked mirror, the quaint motto and the samplers, worked in varicolored yarns and framed. The spotless neatness of the room, which alone

seemed cold and bare, now became the pure
setting for her jewel-like presence. The place
lost its simplicity by the very richness of her
lace fichu flung on the end of the wash-stand,
the rosary of silver beads with its crucifix of
carved ivory, which she laid on the bed, to put
later under her pillow. Near the lace fichu on
the stand she laid her timepiece, her little heap
of rings, and her chatelaine. Over the chair
was her dress of shimmering brocaded silk, the
color of a primrose. The edge of the skirt
was stained and wet, the bodice retained the
gracious lines of her figure, as outer petals
fallen from a rose still hold the curve of the
bud they clothed. She snuffed out one of
the candles, and lay in bed watching the other
one burn, with mournful eyes. She had pushed
back the bed-curtains in order that the air
might be freer. Physically, she was so weary
that after her frame had once relaxed she could
scarcely move or lift her hands from the cov-
erlid. Despite her desire to think over the
events of the long day, her eyelids closed
wearily in profound slumber.

Several hours later she awakened uneasily.
As she opened her eyes, the candle burning
low sputtered into a blue flame and went out.
She had the sensation of one striving to breathe
freely and throw off the suffocating impression
of an evil dream. Raising herself in bed she
looked around her fearfully. The darkness

developed into a real and threatening terror.
The cold sweat broke out over her. Instinctively, unconscious of any motive prompting
the motion, she rose with slow and deliberate
movements as if in a trance, and crossed to
the one casement in her room and swung it
open. It had ceased raining and grown warmer.
A soft, sweet air was blowing. Through the
breaking clouds the full moon appeared high
in the heavens. In the misty silver light the
form of a sentinel pacing the hill-line seemed
of unnatural height. The chain of watch-fires
burned redly. The air blew her hair around
her face, which in her indefinable dread had
acquired that pallor of the flesh more intensely
colorless than the whiteness any inanimate object might possess. With one hand she held
her night-robe together at her throat. The
garment lent her by the Quaker housekeeper
fell in straight, voluminous folds. Her other
hand and arm were stretched forth to keep
open the casement, which swung to and fro
easily at the slightest wind. Her pained and
abstracted gaze was fixed in one direction.
She was dimly conscious that an instinct
stronger than reason bade her wait. Her
heart, which at first had beaten violently and
irregularly, relapsed into slow throbbing. At
last that for which she waited came to pass.
A moan escaped her as she saw emerge from
the black shadow of some distant woods a

figure which moved swiftly across the moonlit field, beyond the rows of huts, but inside the line of the sentinel. She opened her lips to call, but no sound came. The moon was momentarily obscured by a cloud. When the darkness lifted, the figure had disappeared. That slender shadow-like form, led by the semblance of a huge dog — could it have been her brother? No, no; 'twas but the fancy of her restless mind, this ghostlike vision. She leant far out of the window, straining her eyes to see once more those shadowy forms. But only the dark figure of the sentinel regularly pacing his beat met her gaze.

A premonition of evil weighed suffocatingly upon her. She knelt by the little bed in which she had lain down contentedly but a few short hours ago. She clasped the rosary tightly to her breast, the sharp corners of the cross bruising her tender flesh.

"Dear Mother of God," she whispered, "Our Blessed Lady, intercede with thy dear Son for me, that He may remember my brother's blindness, and let him not meet misfortune nor trouble." Sobbingly, she repeated one of the convent prayers. "I compassionate thee, Sorrowing Mary, for the terrors felt by thy anxious heart when thou didst lose thy dear son Jesus. Dear Mother, by thy heart, then so agitated, intercede for me.

Obtain for me the virtue of patience and the gift of fortitude.   Amen."

Even as Mademoiselle de Berny knelt weeping, Heyward, in his hut not far distant, was awakened sharply from the uneasy sleep into which he had fallen after much troubled thought by the knocking over of the table, which fell against his bed.   He sprang to his feet and grasped the intruder.   By the light of the dying fire, despite the moonlit air of the bright night, pouring in the open door, he recognized Armand.   As in his astonishment his grasp relaxed, the boy drew away and flung himself heavily on his bed. Heyward closed the door and prodded the fire, piling on some light wood, which blazed merrily, reflecting its dancing lights in the stream of water which was dripping from the boy's clothing.   He was fully dressed, and must have been out a long time, for the rain had not ceased less than an hour ago.   He seemed to be in a somnambulistic condition, as he lay on the bed with closed eyes, breathing rapidly, one arm flung above his head, the other outstretched with upturned palm, as beseeching something.   But wherever he had been the thing of the moment consisted not in questioning him, but in removing his damp clothing.

" Armand," said Heyward, shaking him gently, " wake up."

But the sleeper seemed insensible to sound

or touch. Having now no doubt that the lad was in a somnambulistic state, Heyward removed his wet clothing as speedily as possible, gashing his left hand on the sword which hung unsheathed at the sleeper's side. He wrapped the boy in a dry blanket taken from his own bed, and, raising the fragile form, forced some brandy between the lips purple with cold. Young Stirling half awakened, choking and sputtering, then as he was allowed to lie down again he turned over on his side and slept.

The young man, partially dressing, seated himself on the bed beside the sleeper, moistening the forehead and lips with brandy, chafing the slender wrists and hands until they grew warm again. Again he felt the old and unconquerable jealousy of the lad's resemblance to his sister. The hands he held so like hers, yet not hers, — the semblance lacking the spirit, — filled him with a repugnance curiously at war with the genuine affection he had for the boy. But her hands! Ah, had he not thought to lay his burning face against her cool and gentle hands, as one might kneel at the shrine of his saint, with fevered brow and smarting eyes pressed against the cold stone! With an effort he continued to rub the helpless hands, now grown quite warm, looking steadfastly at the beautiful face half-turned from him, leaving most prominent the long, oval sweep of the cheek and chin. The hound crouched near his master's head, its bright and intelligent eyes following the young man's movements. Now and then it licked the sleeper's face and hands. At last Heyward put the hands under the blankets, which he drew well up over the boy, and then sought his own bed and sat down at its foot, gazing long into the fire with troubled face. He was roused from his reverie by his companion, who had risen, and, with his hound at his heels, was moving around the room as if in search of something. The blind eyes were open, reflecting the firelight, as Armand felt the clothes Heyward had spread over the chair to dry. He knelt and examined the floor. At last he hit against one of the table legs, and rising passed his hand across the top on which lay his sword. Satisfied, he picked it up and sought his bed again.

Heyward's interest in his companion's movements subsided, absorbed in his deeper thought and painful conjecture as by what means Mademoiselle de Berny had learned of his position in Philadelphia. The fire cast its last flickering lights upon his intent colorless face; the last log of wood sunk into ashes, the flames dying and the crimson embers blackening slowly. But the watcher remained heedless of the dark as well as of the chill air coming in by the door he had forgotten to fasten, and which had blown open.

Chapter VII

THE day following Heyward saw nothing
whatever of Mademoiselle de Berny,
and almost as little of her brother, who
took his meals at headquarters, returning only
to spend the night in the cabin. The young
man deemed it wisest to refrain from mention-
ing his guest's somnambulistic wanderings, as it
might serve no better purpose than to terrify
him and his sister. But he very prudently
fastened the door so securely that it would be
almost impossible for young Stirling to open
it without awakening him. Neither did Mademoiselle de Berny, on her part, mention the
circumstance which lingered hauntingly in her
thought, although she strove to put the ghostly
vision she had seen aside, as the disordered
fancy of a person but half-awake. On the
other hand, it might have been some new
escapade on Armand's part, which he would
make known to her in good time. Delicacy
held her from forcing his confidence. At least
he was safe and with her. She preferred to
put aside the disturbing element, with the instinctive desire to ignore that which seems
intangible and a vague prescience of evil when
no explanation offers itself.

But the question, other than the lad's mid-
night wanderings, over which Heyward brooded
constantly, trying to find some clue to Mademoiselle de Berny's recognition of his official
capacity in Philadelphia, was destined to be
solved for him by one of those curious and
unaccountable flashes of memory, which, suggested by a trifle, as a spark sets a train of
powder ablaze, will illumine what has hitherto
been impenetrably dark. Late in the afternoon of Mademoiselle de Berny's second day
in camp, he was returning from a visit to a
brother officer who lay ill in a nearby farm-
house. He had come into camp again by a
roundabout way. Intending to make a short
cut through a belt of the forest which ran for
some distance along the creek back of headquarters, he entered the bridle-path, walking
slowly with bent head, idly swinging his sword.
The shade of the woods was grateful to him,
for the brightness of the sun served but to
intensify the depression which weighed heavily
upon him. The beauty of the spring day, contrasting with his sad thought of the sick man
he had just left, the keen joyousness of the
earth, heedless of one of her suffering children,
filled him with a profound melancholy. He
sighed heavily. As if in mockery of that sigh,
there came a faint strain of sprightly music.
He paused and listened. The greenness of
the woods was impenetrable, but the music

continued, elusive, gay, sometimes seeming
close, then distant — unsympathetic, as in
laughing derision of pain it stung him as a
mocking word, rousing him irritably from his
apathetic and melancholy mood. With some
curiosity he turned, and parting the branches,
pressed forward in the direction of the sound.
He had proceeded but a few steps, however,
when the trees became scantier, and he caught
a flash of delicate old rose color. At last,
some distance away, the trees formed an archway, making a natural frame for the picture
which presented itself to his gaze. On the
further side of the interlacing branches, arching
green against the blue sky, there was a circle
of unbroken ground. Beyond this the woods
closed in again, but not so thickly, for glimpses
of the gray stone of the headquarters could be
seen. In the open space several people were
moving lightly in time to the music. The
golden sunlight, checkered in places by the
shadows of the leaves, cast its glorifying lustre
upon the careless and merry dancers. He recognized Mademoiselle de Berny in her primrose-
colored gown, her brother, General Von Steuben and his secretary, Lieutenant Walker.
Also there were two young French officers,
who, learning that a country-woman of theirs
was in camp, had hastened to call. Evidently,
they had not found her at headquarters, and
had followed her whither she had gone for a

stroll. Their horses were tied to nearby trees.
An old negro, seated on the stump with his
fiddle, furnished the music. There was one
person needed to complete the set, but the
dancers made shift to change positions at the
proper time, and were no whit disconcerted.
Young Stirling and his dog formed one side
of the minuet. The great hound had been
carefully taught, and it threaded its way intelligently among the dancers. His master
moved with an ease so remarkable that his
dancing seemed rather a spiritual than a material expression of the body. He had a fawn-
like grace, a joyousness of movement which
seemed a reflection of the buoyant spring sea-
son. While Mademoiselle's face was essen-
tially intellectual in its type of loveliness, his
possessed rather a wild-woods intelligence, the
alertness of a young forest creature ready to
spring away at human approach. He cast an
intoxicating spell over the solitary spectator, so
that he found it almost impossible to turn his
gaze upon her toward whom his thoughts ever
tended. Now, as Mademoiselle de Berny
passed alternately from beneath the flickering
shade of the trees into the open sunlight, she
too was not less a part of spring than any
flower, in her primrose gown — the yellow
lace kerchief crossed over her breast and
tied around her slender waist, the miniature
pendent from a chain around her throat,

her dark curls caught in a high knot on her
head.   Like the jingle of tiny bells the feminine trifles hanging on silver chains from the
chatelaine she wore swung against each other,
— a small, sweet, silvery sound, distinct when
the tones of the fiddle softened.   Her partner
was Baron Von Steuben.   Although the little
Prussian was skilled in the ceremonials of the
court as in the manœuvring of an army, yet
his grace was less apparent than his corpulency,
and his good, perspiring face more convincing
of his kindly heart than the gallant attentions
he showered upon the young girl — attentions
which she accepted with so open and arch a
coquetry that, despite his disapproval, her
pretty airs brought a smile to her lover's face,
a smile infinitely tender in its amusement.
How little she realized the suffering and privation and the bitterness which the great body of
soldiers in the encampment yonder bore un-
complainingly.   In France a queen played at
being shepherdess and dairymaid in the Little
Trianon, while a starving populace grew riot-
ous outside her garden.   Now a breath from
that same garden mingled with the free air of
this young country.

On the moss-covered ground the figures of
the dancers swayed and bowed to the minuet.
Absorbed in the rhythmic movements, they
did not observe the solitary spectator leaning
against a nearby tree, until one of the buckles

of Mademoiselle de Berny's shoes snapped and
flew some distance, falling at the young man's
feet. He picked it up and returned it to her
silently, bowing with profound gravity. But
despite his unmoved countenance, his heart
was throbbing tumultuously. For as Mademoiselle de Berny received the buckle from him,
her attitude as she stood with one hand outstretched, the other holding her gown, the design
of the trinket which he recognized and his
own action in returning it,— all revealed to him
in an almost overwhelming flash of memory
the fact that he had met her previous to that
time which he had hitherto deemed his first
acquaintance with her.

The incident, interrupting the dance, ended
it, bringing a sharp realization of the time of
day to Baron Von Steuben, who, bidding a
courtly if hasty adieu to his fair companion,
until he should rejoin her at the supper table,
hurried away to drill a regiment, his stout,
active figure ever a little in advance of his long-
legged secretary, who dragged his lame foot
lazily, and turned with a last wave of his hat to
Mademoiselle who had seated herself on a log.
One of the young Frenchmen knelt to fasten
her buckle again on her shoe. The other
officer brought her cloak, which she had removed during the dance, and put it around her.
Then bidding her farewell, he had gone to
untie the horses of himself and his companion.

Mademoiselle de Berny glanced at Heyward who stood near. His eyes were fixed upon her in a gaze that startled and embarrassed her. She bent her head, directing her entire attention to the young officer kneeling at her feet. But Heyward had lost consciousness .of her presence. Once more he was in France in the glittering ball-room at Versailles. Again he saw the gay figure and blue eyes of Marie Antoinette, the heavy face of Louis Quinze, whose cold eyes reflected none of the merriment around him, as they rested upon the figure which was ever the centre of the brilliant throng, a quaint and simply clad figure in black velvet, with scant, gray locks, unpowdered, falling to the shoulders around a spectacled and benevolent countenance.

This printer of seventy, exchanging the quaint gallantries of poor Richard with the court beauties, was the idol of Paris. The face of the hour vying in popularity with that of the Queen, and which was to be seen on all snuff-boxes and trinkets, was that of the American ambassador, Benjamin Franklin. Louis' dull eyes alone rested unfavorably upon this unpretentious person, as if there were dawning in his slow mind the fact that for a king to assist the subjects of another sovereign who were in open rebellion, was setting a dangerous example which might in time be turned against himself. This envoy, representative of revolutionary and republican sentiment in the New World, was firing the young French nobility with those ideas, leaving him, the sovereign, alone in his resolution to maintain peace with England.

The young man recalling the intense anxiety as to the strength of the King's opposition which weighed upon the hearts of the patriots in Paris at that time, was not amazed that the faces around him had made but dim impression that night when the feeling toward the Insurgents was nearing a crisis and the King's disfavor became apparent even toward the Queen consort who was foremost in fêting Franklin. But now did he recall an abbé, thin, wrinkled, and of great height, with the sharp glance of a wit and the manner of a courtier. On his arm was his niece. Heyward could recall her even less distinctly, retaining a vague impression of having watched her dancing the minuet near him, as he leant against the wall, engaged in conversation with her uncle, striving not to let his anxiety as a patriot become apparent to the subtle abbé, who strongly advocated Louis' policy to maintain amicable relations with Great Britain. The buckle of the young French girl's slipper had snapped and fallen at the American's feet, who had picked it up, and borrowing a knife had tightened the spring, which was slightly sprung. As he held it for her until she should have

finished the dance, he had noted almost mechanically the design of the trinket, which,
curiously, remained his most distinct impression of the ball.   One thing he recalled posi-
tively—the name of the abbé.   Ah, fool that
he had been not to have recognized Mademoiselle as the niece of the Abbé de Berny.
She, meeting him a year later in Philadelphia,
whither she had accompanied her step-father
and his son, must have recognized him as a
young Virginian who that winter had been
closely, although not openly, allied with Franklin at Versailles in the American cause.   His
mission there had been a secret one under the
guise of travelling for study and recreation.
Protected by his family and friends, all stanch
loyalists and ignorant of his position, he had
been enabled, upon his return from abroad, to
spend the winter in Philadelphia engaged in
the secret service of Washington.

"Major Heyward," said the French officer,
"I regret that I must resign to you the honor
of fastening Mademoiselle's buckle.   My fingers have proven all thumbs.   You will pardon me, Mademoiselle," he continued, rising,
"if I leave you so unceremoniously, but my
division must appear at once *au grande parole*.
I fear even now I am late."   He bent and
kissed her hand.   "Adieu, then, until this
evening, when I shall claim a dance at headquarters should His Excellency's mood favor

any social diversion." He rejoined his companion who had already mounted.

Heyward watched them silently until their horses, moving at a brisk canter, disappeared from sight. Then he turned to Mademoiselle. The two seemed alone, despite the fact of young Stirling's presence. He had possessed himself of the negro's fiddle and stood some distance from them trying the strings.

"Listen, Diane," he cried, placing the fiddle under his chin and drawing the bow across. "Now, fellow," he added, addressing the old negro, and seating himself on the ground, "you may dance if you will, although it avails me nothing, for I cannot see. Yet, wait; you may teach me a song of your people. Sit down there, that I may feel you facing me."

The glances of the two overhearing his command met in a smile of mutual sympathy, which, in its unconsciousness of self for the moment, was full of spontaneity and understanding.

"Mademoiselle," said Heyward, seating himself beside her on the log, "in Paris once I had the pleasure of fixing this same buckle for you." His dark eyes were full of warmth. He drew forth his pocket-knife, and opening it, proceeded to mend the trinket. "Just so had the spring sprung before," he continued. "I saw you then, yet such was the anxiety of

my mind at the time, that it was not until I
recognized the design that I remembered."

"To forget was not gallant, Monsieur," she
rejoined softly. She could control her voice
and expression so that they betrayed nothing
of the surprise his words were to her. But
she could not control the quickened heart
throb which sent the blood surging over her
face, and she turned her head from him.

For some time neither spoke. In the mind
of each was the same wonder, marvelling at
the quietude fallen upon them. In secret had
each held long and imaginary conversations
with the other; in secret had each rehearsed
the explaining of bitter words — had each forgiven and been forgiven. And both had felt
a deep despair lest they might never have the
opportunity to right themselves. At last they
were together, alone and undisturbed. Yet
now they felt no need of words. Beyond the
little stream rippling freshly near them, the
meadow rose in long level stretches to a hill-
line merging purple and indistinct into the
paling sky. Along this hill-line passed a flock
of sheep and lambs driven by a boy and a
dog. In the yet further distance an orchard
in bloom made a soft and hazy mass of color.
It was a strangely peaceful and pastoral scene,
seemingly far remote, as of a different age in
a different land from the encampment, where
all was desolate; where even the tender touch

of the spring might not heal the desolate
stumps, and where the bruised grass died beneath the trampling of many feet on the hard
earth worn bare and red. The plaintive negro
melody Armand was singing sounded dreamily
afar. Heyward, forgetting to mend the buckle,
held it idly in his palm ; never should he forget the design — the medallion of a little weeping cupid set around with gold. But a sudden
dread of this strange quietude seized upon
Mademoiselle de Berny.

" It is cold," she said, shivering and moving
along the log to where the sunlight fell. " Has
not the breeze grown chilly ? "

Remembrance had blown like a cold breath
upon her love. She drew her cloak closely
around her. As if an entranced spell had
been broken, her companion's face lost the
dreamy and happy expression which had come
to it, and grew harassed. He felt the deep
and natural anxiety of a young man, confident
that his actions are guided by right principle;
yet knowing that the woman he worships condemns him, is desirous of her good opinion
almost to the temptation of sacrificing his
integrity.

" Mademoiselle de Berny," he said in a low
and troubled voice, " only a very urgent message which it was necessary for me to convey
at once to General Washington kept me from
bidding you farewell in person, but I had writ-

ten to you in explanation. It was not your
accusation at the coffee-house which caused
my flight," his face flushing darkly. "It was
necessary that I should go that afternoon, —
even earlier would have benefited me, — but I
could not miss that last opportunity of seeing
you. The letter I should have handed you
at parting would have explained much; but
in my alarm lest your knowledge of my position might be general, and full of anxiety to
fulfil the commission intrusted to me, the letter was forgotten. Later I discovered my loss.
The letter was returned to me by your brother,
or rather, by General Washington, and I destroyed it. It may be for the best that you
never saw it, Mademoiselle, yet I do not believe you would have judged me so harshly
had you seen it."

"Can't you understand," she cried, "how
I felt? From the first of my meeting you
again in Philadelphia, I suspected your position. Yet I scarcely dared admit it to myself.
But that day, that day in the coffee-house!
To hear General Stirling answering you so
honestly, so sincerely, with no suspicion that
you did not meet him fairly. Was it nothing
to see you appear less manly than he? But
it was not that which angered me so that I
betrayed my knowledge to you afterwards. It
was my horror to see Armand echo what you
said. He, too, to express such sentiments.

The disgrace of it was torturing me. And my uncle nodding to what you said, believing you from the bottom of his heart, his heart innocent as a little child's in its lack of suspicion. But it was above all Armand, Armand in his ignorance and his ambition for fame, seeming to echo only your words and drawing no distinction between his father's brave death in an open fight and the ignoble mission of a spy. Monsieur, I felt I should die of my anger with you, and when you let fall the cup of tea — ah, had you drank that toast, I should never have forgiven you!" She was silent for a moment, exhausted by the intensity with which she had spoken. Then suddenly she put out both her hands to him. Her eyes were wet with tears. " Ah, Monsieur," she cried, " how should a soldier meet his enemy save openly and with unsheathed sword and with fair notice that he approached!"

The appeal went to her listener's heart. Any defence he could make would seem a subterfuge. He bent and kissed her little hands which he had taken in his. " Ah, dear Mademoiselle," he said brokenly, "women cannot understand war."

The softness of the previous moment left her face. She drew her hands from his. " No," she said bitterly, "I cannot understand. An honorable man may not win by base means. Can one touch pitch? I am not unjust, Monsieur, nay, to an extent I respect your attitude, even have I found excuse, saying that in your veins ran a commoner blood, better perhaps and more unselfish than in mine, yet lacking that quality of pride which would make some men refuse to profit by the license of war."

"Mademoiselle," he said patiently, betraying no hurt at her words, only a great anxiety lest she should misunderstand him, "it is doubtless a very fine thing to be cosmopolitan and independent to the extent you admire. But in time of war every man feels his dependence and also the dependence of others upon him. Then is not the time for fine speeches nor for fine gentlemen. Then a man's duty is clearly and simply defined for him. He must stand by the side he has chosen. No longer is he an individual with individual rights. He is but part of a great whole. His sole obligation to society is to remain loyal to his party. It is better then to have a commoner blood than that of so fine a strain as to render a gentleman of no more use than a priest or a woman when his country demands soldiers. Dear Mademoiselle," he added gently, "sometime you will learn that common-sense often proves to be more virtuous than the selfish and obstinate holding to an ideal."

He paused and awaited her reply. But she

made none, turning her head from him so that he saw but the lustrous coils of her hair shadowing one delicate ear and the outline of her cheek and chin. She was, he felt, remote and far from him. The only realities in life were his sick friend, the movements on foot for the next day, the dreary encampment, — love was failing him, — but for comfort, his hand sought the hilt of his sword and rested there.

Mademoiselle de Berny met his abstracted glance in which he showed no consciousness of her presence.

"Monsieur," she said, "Monsieur—" and when she had said that much she paused dumbly, unwitting what to say.

He looked at her inquiringly.

"It was nothing," she said; "I was thinking of something else. I — I scarcely knew what I was saying." She looked away from him. "I wish you would go away," she said. "Why do you trouble me so? I want you to go away." Ashamed of her weakness, unable to control the trembling of her lips, she would not look at him nor say farewell when he rose and left her.

The wind had grown chilly and the sunlight had lost its gold. The stream ran dully at her feet. Nervously she opened and shut the fan which, with other feminine trinkets, hung from the chatelaine around her waist, — a Louis Quatorze fan mounted on mother-of-pearl

sticks, with a painting by Boucher of shepherd-
esses blowing kisses to languishing swains —
fit sceptre of a mincing and effeminate court
wielded by hands of favorites swaying the wills
of kings. This fragile creation, its perfume
breathing of court intrigue and unlicensed
amours, had no place in this young country,
on which was dawning the new republic. In
France, this same fan had been a thing of
power. Here it was a toy, to be used perhaps and cast aside; to be blown away lightly
as a fallen leaf by the new sentiment which,
like the winds of heaven, swept across the
country, bringing new vigor and life. There
was no place for it in this New World, even the
best which it represented. The old-time ideal
of honor befitting a gentleman was scorned,
thought the girl, bitterly recalling Heyward's
words. What was she, save a light and fickle
scion of that Old World whose sentiments he
despised, whose society he flouted. He had
met her at Versailles, and forgotten. But she
had remembered. In her face burned a color
the fan might not cool. She rose and went
over to her brother.

"Come, Armand, it is growing late." She
put her arm around him. "Oh, let us go away,
my dear, my dear; we will leave this America
and go back to France, Armand, — our beautiful France!"

But he pushed her away with the arm which

held the bow. " Listen, Diane! I have caught the tune. And I shall never go back to France. When you go there, I shall not be with you."

Chapter VIII

THE 18th of May is marked in the history of Philadelphia, at the Revolutionary period, as the date of the Mischianza. At Valley Forge the day passed quietly in preparation for an expedition on the morrow to Barren Hill. Through Major Heyward, General Washington had learned of the intention of the British to shortly evacuate Philadelphia. So uncertain, however, was the information which the young man was able to give, as to the near time of this movement, that Washington, to be more exact, ordered the Marquis de La Fayette, with two thousand strong, to cross the Schuylkill and take a position near the city. In Philadelphia, at the same time, the folly of the British was hourly reaching its extreme. Veterans of the army, mortified by the inaction of Howe during the past winter, were doubly chagrined by this exhibition of unlicensed vanity and folly on the part of their commander and those young officers whom his defeat should have most humiliated. Had they not prophesied grimly that the loose discipline of the army was doing more to weaken its power than any battle yet, or to be, experienced? And among these veterans whose choler had been most

apparent was General Stirling. His natural
irritation as a soldier at the condition of military affairs acquired an intensity of feeling from
the fact of his private and personal anxiety as
regarded the welfare of his nephew and Mademoiselle de Berny. True, he had news of
them which was, in its way, ample assurance of
their safety. But secretly he fretted much —
lonely and irritable in their absence. A note,
written by Mademoiselle de Berny and duly
inspected by Washington, had been given to
a young lieutenant about to set out with his
men on a foraging expedition. As instructed,
the officer gave the letter to a farmer going
into town, and the countryman conveyed the
missive to General Stirling. The old soldier
re-read the note many times, shaking his head
dubiously as Mademoiselle de Berny explained
briefly her following Armand to Valley Forge,
taking much complacent and pleasant credit to
herself for the intuition which had guided her
so wisely, and speaking naught of any motive
which had inspired Armand to go to the
rebels' camp beyond a spirit of adventure.
Richard Heyward's name was not mentioned.
And with a last assurance that General Washington, who was a kindly host, would return
herself and her brother to Philadelphia as soon
as it was expedient, and the journey could be
taken safely, she enclosed her very dutiful respect and love.

"Ah, Diane," said the soldier, placing the non-committal little note in his breast pocket, "ye harry up my feelings sorely. Fain would I be to clip your pretty wings, and send ye back to France to stay until this war is over. Though ye would naught confess it, my girl, I fear me that that young rebel who served us so neat a trick in slipping away has somewhat to do with this journey. Back to France ye go for this trick, Diane, though it tear my heart-strings. But with one eye on the war, the other of mine orbs is not enough to keep guard o'er ye, lest ye marry some worthless scalawag who betrayeth his king."

At the great ball in the evening, General Stirling was one of the few officers who appeared in full-dress uniform, wandering disconsolately from corner to corner, satisfied only in finding some old comrade who would listen sympathetically to his contemptuous comments on the fair ladies and knights swaying to the stately measure of the minuet, with gay abandonment to the pleasure of the moment and scornful of any adverse criticism. The only thing which had made the thought of the entertainment endurable to him was the pleasurable anticipation it had afforded Mademoiselle de Berny. He recalled the delight with which she had shown him the gown to be worn upon this occasion. Had she not refused to have any knight but him? In his secret heart the old

soldier had pictured himself with the lovely
and girlish figure at his side, slowly prome-
nading the ball-room ; he, who was childless,
lavishing on her the pride and affection he
would bestow on a daughter, vain of her
accomplishments and beauty, whereas he would
have blushed at praise of his own valor and
prowess. It was this disappointment to his
loving pride, when like an over-foolish parent
he would have seen her first among those
Philistines he flouted, which hurt him sorely.
Curiously enough he had no feeling regarding
the fact of her leaving him, heedless of the
anxiety which would be his. A lonely and
middle-aged man, never having had wife or
child, he had cherished in his heart a secret
ideal of his daughter — the daughter who had
been his only in fancy until Mademoiselle de
Berny came to fill that sacred place, and receive the tenderness of a pathetic love which
had heretofore found no outlet. He left the
ball-room at an early hour and went to his
quarters, veiling his loneliness under a masque
of surliness, which made his presence more to
be shunned than desired. Had not Diane's
absence made the day and evening doubly a
mockery and doubly distasteful to him ?

But the ball went on merrily, despite the
prediction of the gloomy old general and his
especial cronies seated smoking their pipes
under the starlit sky on the upper balcony

of a stately Philadelphian home, while to their unwilling ears came the sound of dance music. The revellers' laughter filled the soft spring air, blowing sweet across what had once been "Penn's faire greene countrie town," but was now a captive city, filled by swaggering red-coats, with its stateliest hômes made the army quarters, with Old World follies and vices running riot, while gambling and drinking halls flourished, and officers fought duels in this city of the peace-loving Quakers. And as he sat smoking his pipe grimly, General Stirling fell to dreaming waking dreams. Soft as the touch of a baby's hand on his warrior face his hope of a home in old England with his adopted children soothed his troubled mind. Diane should have her heart's desire. Did she want her lilies? He would find her fields of them wherein she might gather all she would, he told himself, calling the lilies by their sweet old English name of flower-de-luce.

Since early morning had this day's fête continued. Entitled the *Mischianza*, — an Italian word signifying *medley*, — it was without doubt the most magnificent display of folly ever held in America. Given in honor of the retiring commander, Lord Howe, it seemed a proper finish to the frivolities and sensualities of the British in Philadelphia. During the day a regatta and mock tournament had been enacted,

and the participants continued to wear the cos-
tumes of the tournament, appearing thus dressed
at the ball in the evening. But few uniforms
were to be seen, and they appeared strangely
incongruous in this assemblage. The knights
of the Blended Rose were dressed in white
and pink satin, with hats of pink silk and
white feathers. The knights of the Burning
Mountain were attired in black and orange.
Each knight had his squire bearing a shield
and spear. Of the women, all gayly attired in
the colors of their respective knights, none
were wives or sisters of the British officers.
They were American women, resident in Philadelphia, whose appearance at this ball drew
forth bitter condemnation from the Continental Army and its sympathizers. So high
did this sentiment run that when the Americans regained possession of the city there was
a heated discussion as to whether these same
young women should be invited to attend the
Whig ball; but the gallantry of General Arnold, so soon to marry into a Tory family,
and, alas, to turn traitor, prevailed, and these
same fickle dames appeared in full force at
the later ball. For this memorable evening
of the Mischianza, the ball-room had long been
in preparation. The walls and ceilings, which
were blue panelled with gold, were adorned
with festoons of pink, crimson, and yellow
roses, which some young officers, under the

K

direction of Major John André, had passed
hours in painting. Half-way up the walls
from the floor, sixty large mirrors reflected
the gay scene. Great branches of wax-lights
added a wonderful brilliancy. As some reck-
less masque — an abandonment of folly and
magnificence — did this dance seem. Had the
officers lost all self-respect, that in time of war
and great distress they cast aside their uniforms to attire themselves foppishly in satins
and feathers, forgetting their own wives and
sweethearts in the mother-country for these
pleasure-loving Whig ladies, passing over
lightly the grave rebuke implied by their
commander's recall to England? Early in
the evening — before ten o'clock — a young
Whig lieutenant, with a company of Dragoons, sought to break up the party by firing
the abatis at the north of the city, which
connected the line of the British redoubts.
Out on the great verandah of the building in
which they were crowded came the knights
and ladies, like some fairy pageant in the
moonshine and the light streaming out from
the casements of the ball-room. The breeze
blew the silver and gold gauze veils, streaming from the powdered hair of the fair Dul-
cineas, as they leant forward, watching the
flames — masses of orange light against the
deep blue sky. The roll-call sounded along
the line, and the guns of the redoubts thun-

dered forth ominously. Little recked the
ladies that the hearts of their knights were
perturbed beneath the white satin waistcoats
the while their gallantry caused them to ap-
plaud with their companions, lest the latter
suspect that the brilliant illumination and the
firing were not at all a part of the celebration.
And as the flames died down and they returned once more to the dance, all unaware
were they of a merry canter, when horse flew
by horse from out Philadelphia in pursuit of
the incendiaries. And on these horses were
mounted many of the veterans of the British
Army, General Stirling leading in the mad
chase. Overhead was the sky glittering with
the stars and moon; their horses' feet seemed
but to touch the springy earth. Far afield
the unbroken moonlit stretch of country across
which they rode, a moving shadow indicated
the fleeing Whigs. Now and then came back
a faint, far call of defiance, which was caught
up by the lusty British and sent pealing back
again.

Little thought General Stirling that among
those whom he pursued was his nephew. The
adventure was not a perilous one; the wonderful clear beauty of the night and the entreaties
of Armand, as he passionately begged permission to accompany the expedition, had caused
Heyward, who was one of the leaders, to
mount the lad on his own horse, while he,

securing another mount, guided his own and his companion's horse. Glancing back, he saw the British had dropped behind and evidently ceased pursuit; he looked at his companion and was glad he had brought him, so exultantly joyous was the lad. His fair hair had become unloosened, and hung waving to his shoulders with a sheen of silver on it from the moonlight. In his white delicate face, his eyes seemed large and black, revealing no lack of intelligence. His slender figure was seated erectly. The Great Dane kept close at the horse's side. It was as if the height of the boy's ambition had been reached. Never before in his life had he been so joyous, never again should he be so!

It was nearly twelve o'clock when they reached Valley Forge. Mademoiselle de Berny had retired hours ago and was sleeping sweetly, unwitting of the merry adventure of her brother. And in Philadelphia the dance went on merrily, the officers since the interruption abandoning themselves recklessly to the pleasure of those rose-wreathed hours.

Between four and five o'clock in the morning doors, hitherto artfully concealed by flowers, were opened, disclosing a dining-room of magnificent proportions. As the gay company entered this room, headed by Lord Howe and his lady, the barbaric splendor of the scene gained its completing touch as the dancers

passed between eighty black slaves in Oriental
dress, with silver collars and bracelets, arranged
in two lines and bowing to the ground. In
this room were two tables reaching from one
end to the other and loaded with pyramids of
jellies, sillabub, cakes, and sweetmeats. At
the conclusion of the supper the herald of the
Blended Rose, whose side had won in the
tournament, entered in his habit of ceremony,
of rose-red satin and silver lace, and proclaimed
the King's health, the Queen's, and those of the
royal family, and of Lord Howe and his lady,
the army and navy and their respective com-
manders, the knights and their ladies. Each
of these toasts was followed by a flourish of
music. And at the last the company rose and,
amid the clinking of wine glasses, sang "God
Save the King," while the wax candles burned
low and the rose of pleasure faded beneath the
disillusionizing light of day. The sober reality
of war was to end this gorgeous pageantry for
the British officers, and the pricking of their
consciences make the remembrance of the fes-
tivities a sore spot in the memories of the Whig
damsels.

At the same time, but twenty miles distant,
two thousand men in ragged uniforms stood
with bowed heads receiving the benediction of
their chaplain. The gray light of dawn fell
harshly on the grim faces marked by privation
and irking care, the hollow cheeks mostly dark

with a heavy beard. Their gaunt features wore an expression of stoicism, neither elation nor despair. But the eager piercing eyes were full of dauntless fire. For these men there was nothing left to fear. They had known the worst. The past terrible winter they had been called upon to endure all that seemed unendurable. Their bare feet had left bloody prints upon the snow. They had known nakedness and starvation; they had been stricken by disease and had seen their comrades dying from exposure. Their beloved commander had been reviled. More than possible failure ever stared them in the face. The liberty for which they endured, as well as fought, seemed ever to fly from them, eluding their eager grasp which closed upon air. Over their heads, as the sword suspended by a single hair, hung the threat of abject slavery in case of failure. But grimly, without a sigh for their dark lot, as the bleak winter world cherished the eternal promise of spring, so did the stern blood of the Puritan fathers flowing in their veins remind them that the Lord did not leave his righteous ones to perish. Their constant prayer of endurance had arisen: "Oh, Lord, how long wilt thou look on! Deliver my soul from the sword; my darling from the power of the dog; save me from the lion's mouth; from the wicked that oppress me; from my deadly enemies who compass me

about.   Keep me as the apple of the eye,
hide me under the shadow of thy wing."

And so, with the melting of the snows and
the budding of the trees, spring had returned ;
and as its warm, sunny smile caused the breaking up of the ice-bound rivers, so had the
flood-gates of bitterness and stoicism in these
men's hearts opened to the on-rushing tide of
hope which reflooded and inspired them.   As
the troops formed, there was to be seen none
of the pomp and circumstance of war, but good
muscle and vigorous action and the swinging
stride of hardened men.   Under a cluster
of trees stood a little group of women, composed of Lady Washington and the wives of
some of the officers.   Mademoiselle de Berny
was also one of the group.   Her brother had
wandered nearer the troops.   He sat, a sightless,
eager listener, at the foot of a giant oak, his
arm around the neck of his hound, the two
faces pressed together.   The lad's hair, with
its peculiar ash-yellow tint, seemed the color
of a flower.   He had had but a few hours'
sleep, and his pallor showed him to be exhausted from the hard ride of the night just
drawing to a close.   The imposing figure of
His Excellency, on his white horse, was seen,
first here and then there, as he surveyed the
soldiers.   The first sun-rays struck sharply
through the trees.   But there were no brilliant
uniforms to glitter in the light.   There was

heard no martial music to quicken the cours-
ing of the blood. But there was a flash of
color as a regiment of Indian warriors stepped
into line, their painted bodies glistening, their
heads gayly adorned with nodding feathers.
From amidst a body of mounted officers, there
moved out one soldier, bearing aloft a white
standard with the gold fleur-de-lis. A prolonged huzza arose.

They were the French lilies.

Mademoiselle de Berny's hands were involuntarily pressed against her throbbing heart.
Did she not recognize the manly figure in its
uniform of buff and blue, the impetuous backward fling of the handsome powdered head as
the soldier removed his hat? It was Major
Heyward. The horse, with its satiny head,
its quivering nostrils, and slender legs, seemed
a part of the youth and grace embodied in the
rider. Across the intervening troops the
young man's gaze fell upon a girl's figure in
a brown Quaker cloak. Beneath her proud
gaze he saw shining a deep and shy regard.
With instinctive humbleness, an answering shyness springing up within himself, he looked
away. The huzzas rose again, swelling louder
on the fresh morning air to the cry of the
French officers caught up by the Americans,
"Vive la France!"

But there was one soldier who heard the
triumphal shouting only as a din above which

he listened to the whisper of an unspoken love.
Where others saw the gleaming of white satin,
he was reminded of the immaculate honor and
purity shining in worshipped eyes ; where the
embroidered lilies glittered like gold to the
gaze of the soldiers, he saw forming the match-
less hues of a fairer flower of France.

Far down the road, as the troops moved on,
Mademoiselle de Berny watched the waving
banner with dreaming eyes, unconscious that
the rest of the women with whom she had
been standing had moved away, leaving her
alone. She saw her brother approaching, his
hand resting on the hound's head, who was
leading him toward her.

"Diane," said the boy, passing his hand
over her face to assure himself that it was she,
" I'm so hungry. Let us go in now to breakfast. Then afterward we will go back to the
tree over there, where we will spend the day.
The moss is like velvet, is it not, Little
Brother?" he added, stroking the hound's
head ; "and you will like it as well as I, old
lazy-bones, to cushion yourself on. Diane,
I get so tired, and I ache so from the bed
I have here. 'Tis naught but straw on boards,
although Major Heyward lets me have all the
blankets."

He put his arm around his sister's neck,
and rubbed his cheek against hers, laughing.

" I should not tell my father that if he were

here, Diane.   He would say, 'Fie, fie, a fine
soldier you would make, my lad, if you can't
stand camp life, and complain about a hard
bed.   Suppose you had to sleep on the frozen
ground, as many have to do!'   That's what
he'd say, Diane."

They spent the greater part of the day out
of doors beneath the tree of which Armand
had spoken.   He amused himself by making
excursions into the neighboring woods and
gathering wild flowers, which he would arrange
with marvellous grace and dexterity, as if their
subtle fragrance and form guided his fingers
more surely than the sight of the blossoms
could have done.

The camp was quiet.   The languor of the
soft spring day rested on all.   There was the
air of relaxed discipline to be seen in an army
prepared to break camp, and move on at once
in obedience to orders, but waiting idly day
after day for summons.   But little signs of
activity were to be seen.   From the chimneys
rose the thin bluish puffs of smoke of the fires
by which the soldiers prepared dinner.   Now
and then parties of men, yoked together to
carts of their own contrivance, were to be seen
dragging wood and provisions from the store-
house to their huts.   In the fields detachments
were being drilled by General Von Steuben.
Young Stirling, becoming tired, lay down upon
the moss, his head pillowed on the Great

Dane's back. The checkered sunlight lay
upon him in flecks of gold and shone brightly
in his open eyes. In those sightless eyes so
blank and glassy Mademoiselle de Berny saw
as in a mirror the shifting reflections of the
leaves overhead against the blue sky, her own
fair and wistful face in miniature. The remembrance of the shadowy figure she had seen
crossing the field the first night of her stay at
Valley Forge came back hauntingly to her,
with a prescience of evil. Yet she lacked
the courage to mention the circumstance to
her brother. As a child, delicate, reserved
and haughty, he seldom took any one into
his confidence, sometimes doing things in a
strangely secretive way, most pitifully apparent
to the great seeing world, but of this latter fact
he was unconscious. Early in life Mademoiselle de Berny had recognized this trait as the
instinctive and pathetically suspicious attitude
of the blind. But there were times when not
even her perfect comprehension of this could
render her impassive to the hurt done her
tender love by his lack of trust. Ah, how
many times had her own eloquent gaze rested
upon his blind eyes with the burning desire
that once, once only if no more, they might
meet hers with understanding and she see his
soul shining in them! Ah, to draw aside the
curtain of his blindness and look down into his
heart! But his affliction separated them as a

screen, so slight that through it might be heard
the beating of their hearts, but so impenetrable
that they could not see each other.   When, as
a little boy he had fallen asleep, content only if
she were beside him, then he had seemed most
hers.   Then the shut white lids veiled the
sightless eyes and he was like other children,
tangible and human in slumber.   So she
would watch him with the fancy in her heart
that the lids would open and reveal bright and
intelligent eyes.   Her anxiety to know the
truth of the incident of the other night deepened.   In the hound's honest gaze she seemed
to see an intelligence struggling for expression.
They were strangely mated, these two, thought
the girl sadly, Armand and the dog he termed
Little Brother, the one who could speak but
might not see, the other, the dumb friend
whose eyes served for two.

At her brother's request she began to tell
him her oft-repeated stories of legendary
heroes, and of actual men who had lived or
died bravely.   Always after she had read or
talked to him for a little while, he would
interrupt, commanding her to speak of his
father.

"He was very brave, Armand," she would
begin.

"I know," the lad would rejoin eagerly.

"And he loved a good joke."

"I remember," he would laugh, "and the

time he and I sewed the sleeves of your dress
up. How it rained that afternoon, and I was
sick. I do not like the storm, Diane. It is
so lonely. I can tell every time it is going to
thunder. It makes me shake all over. How
I cried that afternoon, and my father would
make me laugh. You were cross because of
the joke. But my father made you laugh,
too."

"Yes, dear," she would rejoin, "and I tore
my dress trying to get into it. What broad
shoulders your father had. He used to carry
you around perched up on one when you were
a little fellow."

But this afternoon, although she waited for
him to continue the familiar conversation, he
remained silent.

"Diane," he said at last, "my father was
sad because I was blind. I heard him say
once it would not have mattered had I been a
girl, but I was his only son."

"Yes, dear," she said cheerily, although the
tears rushed to her eyes, "that was why your
father loved you so — because you were his
only son."

"Do you suppose it hurt him to die,
Diane?"

"He died like a soldier, Armand."

"Diane," he said, fingering his sword lov-
ingly, "do you think he knows that I am a
prisoner of war? Perhaps, Diane," he said

very softly, reaching for her hand, "it is not necessary that one should fight to serve one's king."

He lay smiling, and at last laughed outright from the delight of his secret thoughts.

"Ah, Diane," he joked, "what do women know of war?"

Chapter IX

THE night fell calm and beautiful. There was no moon, but the starlight was brilliant, filling the air with a white radiance. At Barren Hill the Continental troops slept, some few of the soldiers wrapped in blankets, but the majority lying on the bare ground. The air was warm and soft as that of summer. The murmur of the Schuylkill River was softened by distance. The gray stone walls of the two or three houses, the school building, the old church of St. Peter's, which buildings alone composed the settlement, were softly defined in the starlight. Far away as red sparks showed the watch-fires of Valley Forge. An equal distance to the south lay Philadelphia. In the shadow of the wall of the old church lay the graveyard. On and about the headstones several young officers had spread their blankets, and sat smoking and conversing in low tones. Major Heyward was of the party. He had stretched his blanket on the long soft grass, and leant back against the church wall, but half-listening to the conversation of his companions, as he smoked leisurely with careful attention given to the red glow in the bowl of his pipe. He found

143

himself endeavoring to spell out an inscription on a headstone of white marble almost
sunken in the ground and half-covered by
moss.   With idle interest he leant forward to
see the words plainly, which as he read them
breathed a pathos that stirred his heart with
pity : —

Here lyes Buried ye Body
of Anne, wife to one William Chew,
Who Departed this Life, Dec*br;* 10th, Anno Domini
1705 in ye 20th year of her age
leaving to mourn her, her Husband
and her Two Lyttel Children.

He read the inscription musingly, picturing
the life of this woman long faded to dust, who
in her short years had lived much of life.   He
had a curious fancy that near the boundary of
the spirit land her soul must hover, as one not
content with what death had wrought, beseeching once more entrance to the world as having
therein all claim to earthly happiness.   To
have been cut down in the flower of her youth
— yet she had known somewhat of the fulness
of life.

Through his mind ran the undercurrent of
his thought regarding Mademoiselle de Berny.
She was older by two years than the dead
woman ; but the one was wife, mother, and
dead, while the other was a girl, young, joyous,
with life untried, further removed by lack
of experience from the poor young mother

so long dead than by any stretch of years.
He looked up at the serene sky. The night
kindly to lovers filled his heart with hope,
bringing him conviction that the day would
dawn when she should understand fully all
that which now seemed so unforgivable and
beyond the pale of honor to her.

A great tenderness swept over him. The
life of this buried woman was such as his
mother might have led — a stern hard life, bat-
tling with crushing realities. That this dead
woman, that his own ancestors had borne such
hardships, seemed in no wise a pitiable thing
save for the slight pathos the inscription had
awakened in him. The stern blood of the
Puritan fathers ran purely in him. To endure
for principle, to sacrifice all to the right, seemed
but the natural mode of living. From these
women Mademoiselle de Berny was remote as
some rare flower plucked in a foreign land.
The passionate tenderness of his love for her
knew but one desire — that she might never
know pain nor sorrow. Truly, had these other
women proven themselves "as gold which is
tried." But she was not of that quality ; not
one made to be enduring and strong, but lovely,
fair, and to be protected. For her was to be
no fiery ordeal ; of no heroic metal was she
made ; but she was most perfect in herself
— a flower which would droop beneath the
blazing sun ; her exquisite charm, like the sun-

lit dust of the butterfly's wing or the purple
bloom of the grape, would vanish at the rude
touch.

From his breast pocket he drew the buckle
of her shoe, which he had unconsciously retained the other day on leaving her. The
gold glittered palely in the starlight ; the design of the medallion he could see but faintly,
a mere suggestion of the little weeping cupid.
He turned the trinket over in his palm to
where her name and the date were engraved
on the back.

"Ah, my beautiful Diane," he murmured,
"I wish there existed neither tyranny nor
oppression in the world, and that my country
were at peace! Then might I live quietly with
you ; then might I teach you, that courage
which risks the lives of others to further personal glory is but vanity ; that pride in virtue
is too often self-righteous, grasping the sub-
stance and losing the spirit."

Very early in the morning, as the mists
lifted from the river, scarlet coats could be
seen advancing through the trees in the distant
forest. It was then that the Marquis de La
Fayette made the serious mistake which threatened to involve the entire Continental troops.
What was really the British advance, he believed to be a troop of American Dragoons,
who wore scarlet uniforms. It was not until
he perceived, on the extreme left, more red-

coats that his danger became apparent to him ; and, to the right, another column was seen advancing. The enemy, marching at night, moving rapidly and quietly, had approached within a mile of Barren Hill.

Upon the peaceful air thundered the alarum guns of Valley Forge, warning La Fayette, hoarse, booming, menacing. From his post of watching, eight miles away, on the hilltop at Valley Forge, Washington was observing, through a field-glass, the distant operations. Motionless as a silhouette against the sky, His Excellency's massive form, on his white horse, was to be distinguished some way apart from his officers, who conversed in low tones and with perturbed glances cast upon the majestic figure of their commander, whose face was frozen into a silence none dared disturb. The dignity of his bearing was such that those of his staff who were American officers and had seen La Fayette given promotions to which they were most justly entitled, grew ashamed, and their jealous murmurings that some one else than this French boy should have been sent out, died away. Perhaps it was then that Washington suffered the last and most bitter trial of the past winter, and a black despair filled his heart. For this had his men dragged through those mournful months, — to have the flower of his army in great danger, threatening an absolute collapse of the remaining troops, now in that weak condition which the least thing would shatter.

Now he caught glimpses of the buff and blue uniforms of the Continental soldiers advancing towards the enemy. The intention of the young Marquis to meet an enemy vastly superior in force was suicidal. Battle seemed imminent. In another moment the command was given for the remainder of the army at Valley Forge to form in marching order. His Excellency intended to send out reinforcements.

But suddenly, from under cover of the forest on the northern side of Barren Hill, Washington saw through his field-glass the Continental troops step forth, moving briskly up the river road towards Valley Forge.

The Marquis de La Fayette's manœuvre became apparent to his anxious commander. The buff and blue uniforms seen in the woods belonged to small parties ordered to present themselves as the head of the attacking columns, thus deceiving the antagonist while the main troops beat a hasty retreat and were nearing the ford as the enemy, pausing, prepared to give battle.

Up to this time the British had remained silent, but now there burst upon the fresh morning air strains of martial music — resonant, triumphant. Silently, swiftly, the American troops had moved along the river road until they reached the ford and had crossed to the other side. Then they swung off their hats, and raising their heads, wet though they were, hungry, defeated in their original plan of action, yet glorying in their escape, they gave vent to a prolonged huzza, which well-nigh split their throats — an huzza, clear, defiant, exultant, drowning and ending at once the British music.

From Valley Forge the guns pealed forth again, no longer in ominous warning, but thundering defiance.

His Excellency's compressed lips opened to an inarticulate sound between a groan of relief and a choking sound of triumph.

"It is the ragged fellows," he cried, handing his field-glass to an officer; "the ragged fellows who carry the day!"

A young officer of the Continental troops, making his way cautiously along a bridle path, threading the woods at Barren Hill, paused to listen — a grim smile on his face as he comprehended the triumphal shouting. Then he moved on, with careful outlook for any enemy, conscious of the rashness of the venture which imperilled his freedom for the sake of a woman's trinket. Wakened suddenly from deep slumber that morning, Heyward had forgotten the buckle of Mademoiselle de Berny's shoe, not discovering his loss until later. He was confident that it had slipped

from his pocket during sleep, and probably
lay on the ground where he had been. A
member of one of the patrols which had ridden
out to deceive the antagonists, his party had
engaged in a bloodless skirmish with some
British Dragoons encountered at a cross-roads.
In the skirmish he was separated from his companions, who had been able to follow closely
upon the heels of La Fayette, and had made
the retreat in safety.

Thus, thrown as it were upon his own resources, and with only himself for whom to be
responsible, he determined to make an effort
to recover the buckle. He had passed along a
path seldom used and in the densest part of
the woods, which sheltered him from the observation of the red-coats. At last, reaching
the hill, he had led his horse half-way up the
slope and tied him to a tree. He deemed it
wiser to make the rest of the way alone. But
a dash into the church-yard, where it was
doubtless safe, for the enemy had not as yet
ascended the hill, a moment in which to search
for the buckle, and then a run for his horse.
True, the British might sight and pursue him.
But with his sword and Mademoiselle's buckle
in his breast pocket as a talisman against harm,
and his good horse given loose rein, he could
well afford to fling defiance in the very teeth
of his enemy. And the adventure was a right
merry one. Above the hilltop as he climbed

he could see the tall church steeple with its
gilt cross glittering against the blue sky. The
cross, emblem of papacy to him, reminded him
of Mademoiselle de Berny, Mademoiselle wearing the rosary, which stood for her religion,
living purely, clinging with dauntless and child-
like faith to her ideals, and bidding him also
reach her supreme height serene and aloof from
the struggle and tear of worldly life he must
lead among men, as this cross was. It pointed
to the peace of heaven, as if beneath it existed
not the violent passions of men pitted against
one another in deadly struggle.

Around him on all sides was the dense wood
of the steep hillside, the undergrowth making
the greenness impenetrable, so that he could see
but a few feet ahead of him. Wood flowers —
wild, frail children of the forest — waxed pale
and delicate in the shade. They, too, made
him think of Mademoiselle, as indeed everything beautiful did, or, he reflected pushing
apart the undergrowth where it grew high on
the unfrequented path, as also everything
which was not so recalled her by reason of
the contrast it afforded to her perfection.
His thought was none the less tender for his
amusement as he reflected how all things
centred around her — events in his past life,
once important, now acquiring significance
only as they served to date back from the time
when he had met her. He pushed aside a

heavy bough hanging low and concealing the path in front of him.

"'My lovely maid, I've often thought,'" he hummed, stopping abruptly a second later and raising his musket quickly to his shoulder. Where another path crossed the one by which he had come, stood a Quaker with his back turned to him. He had not heard Heyward approach, being absorbed in watching something visible to him alone at the foot of the hill through a gap in the trees.

The recognition of the unwieldy huge figure, of the profile half-turned from him, and expressive only of coarseness and cunning aroused in Heyward a revulsion of feeling so intense that he paled from emotion. The man he knew to be a paid spy of the British, a nature of the utmost malignity masking its mission beneath the meek garb of the Friends. The fellow leant forward, his expression of interest intensifying.

It was impossible for the young man to retreat. Neither did he desire to do so. Taking a swift step forward, he covered the Quaker with his musket. A twig snapped beneath his foot. The man turned, startled, and retreated a foot or two as he perceived the hostile attitude of the young man whom he recognized. The threat of the musket served for words between the two men, whose enmity had flamed up at the encounter. The Quaker, endeavoring to speak, opened and shut his mouth dumbly several times. The cold sweat came out in drops on his countenance, and his breathing could be heard as if drawn in pain. His pink, sleek countenance became white and flabby, his weak eyes blinking continuously behind his spectacles.

As Heyward commenced speaking, his voice was drowned by a sudden burst of noise, — mad calls and yells, a medley of shrieks, the guttural voices of Indians mingling with calls for reinforcement from the British. A reconnoitring party of red-coats were moving stealthily around the hill, while the regiment of Indians of the Continental Army, which had been cut off by some British Dragoons from accompanying La Fayette, were endeavoring to follow his retreat. Creeping on their hands and knees to avoid being seen, the Indians had suddenly met the enemy face to face, to the dire confusion of both parties. This prospective skirmish was that which the Quaker had been absorbed in watching when Heyward came upon him. The young man, catching a glimpse of the Indians, rightly guessed the cause of the confusion. Realizing his imminent danger, should any of the red-coats seek to escape by rushing up the hill, he ascended to the top hastily, keeping the Quaker ahead of him, with his musket pressed against the prisoner's back. Fortunately the path led to the rear of the old

church, the stone wall of which was greatly
sunken; the back door was torn off its hinges.
Heyward, hearing the guns for the recall of
the reconnoitring parties being fired repeatedly
and imperatively, signifying the return march
of the enemy, was confident that the red-coats,
while they might pass through the settlement,
were not likely to pause for close investigation
of any building.   Another chance also remained
to him, that of making a dash for his horse,
mounting and running the risk of being pursued.   But to seize this opportunity was to
abandon his original purpose, and also set at
liberty a dangerous enemy to the American
cause.

The interior of the building, being like some
great empty barn, had nothing churchly about
it, save where above the dismantled altar the
sunshine fell through the broken stained glass
window in a glory of rose and purple and green
light.   Near the main entrance, opening on the
street, stood the baptismal font, its marble
nicked and broken, and its bowl long turned
into a drinking trough for horses.   One of the
front doors had been torn from its hinges and
lay on the floor of the church.   Long ago the
pews had been taken away.   In one corner a
pile of straw showed that some one had lately
occupied the building.   Doubtless some of the
Continental soldiers had slept there the night
just past.   Great cobwebs hung in the corners

and stretched across the shuttered casements
through which pierced fine rays of dusty golden
light. The brick floor had sunken in places,
and in these spots puddles of water appeared
and moss spread out greenly.

Heyward marched his prisoner into the least
conspicuous corner, and awaited further developments. But as none came after what seemed
an interminable period of inaction on his part,
but which was in reality less than twenty
minutes, he ventured to go to the front door,
keeping a vigilant survey of his prisoner.
As he expected, the tiny street was deserted.
The one or two families inhabiting the place
were Friends, and had barricaded themselves
in their houses. Across the road walked a
dog, carrying a hen it had just killed. Heyward spoke sharply, and the animal, dropping
its prey, slunk off, its tail between its legs.
Not daring to reveal himself uniformed as he
was, at the risk of being seen by some chance
observer, the young man ordered his companion to step half-way outside the doorway and
pick up the fowl. As the Quaker, obeying,
drew back, several British who had climbed
the hill appeared at the end of the road.
Heyward caught a bare glimpse of them and
realized that they in their turn must have had
full view of the Quaker. Without a moment's
hesitation, he ordered the fellow to stand half
within the doorway, so that he himself, con-

cealed from the street behind the closed half
of the entrance, was still enabled to keep his
prisoner under cover of his musket.   He will-
ingly ran the risk of discovery with Mademoiselle's buckle at stake and with an avenue of
escape left open through the rear door of the
church.   The voices of the soldiers became
distinct.

"'Tis a fine place for a May-day picnic,"
one man said jovially; "but, beshrew me, comrades, if 'tis not the rebels' picnic this time.
'Twould not be to my liking to be near His
Lordship Howe in his present tantrum."

"An' did ye hear o' the supper he is to
give to-night?" chuckled another.   "Ha, 'tis
poor relish he will have!   Eh, men, did ye
not hear o' his inviting the fine ladies to sup
with the French stripling who's to be shipped
to England?"

His words were greeted with a loud guffaw.

"Ho, ho, my pious friend," continued the
last speaker, who brought up the rear of the
party and who glanced sharply at the Quaker.
"Ye sent your news a little tardy.   We should
have arrived here before the break o' day, that
we might be on the rebels before they sighted
us."

He burst into hearty laughter.

"Look ye, men, at the sly dog.   While we
went for the rebels, he made his capture at the
chicken-coop.   Ha, ha, the sly dog!   Give me

a Quaker, I say, comrades, for preferring a full
stomach and a lengthy prayer to glory."

The Quaker essayed to answer, stuttering
in his fear, the sweat running down his flabby
face, his hand clutching convulsively the neck
of the chicken.   He felt the threat conveyed
by the musket pressed against his side.   Did
he convey by word or sign the presence of
his captor, he would be a dead man.   Yet
there was a fair chance, should he drop suddenly to the ground or draw quickly aside
and run.   His captor, engrossed in his own
escape, would not have time to deal vengeance.   But his will was paralyzed by terror.
Cowardice bound him to the spot as securely
as iron chains while his one opportunity vanished.

"Ye missed a rare sight, Friend Broadbrim,"
said another man.   "We chased some Indians
to the river, and had a chance o' picking off
a dozen or more as they swam across, their
heads bobbing up and down like corks."

Heyward swore softly under his breath as
he heard the news.

One of the soldiers made a grab at the hen.
But the Quaker clutched it desperately, as if
on it hung his salvation.   How far the matter would have gone was not determined.   A
mounted officer, appearing from the opposite
direction, called sharply to the laggards.   He
glanced at the Quaker and, recognizing him,

nodded briefly, and, wheeling his horse around in front of the soldiers, ordered them to hasten.

Some time elapsed before Heyward dared venture out into the street and go around the church corner into the grave-yard. In all the settlement there was no sign of human being, with the exception of himself and his prisoner. At the extreme further end of the little street, the dog they had seen sat in the middle of the dusty road observing their motions.

As the young man had supposed, the buckle was found near the tombstone, bearing the inscription he had read during the previous night. He did not risk relaxing his vigilance of the Quaker by bending to pick up the buckle, but ordered him to do so, annoyed, however, at the necessity of having the trinket touched by profane hands. Then, keeping the man in front of him and keenly on the alert for any sign of the enemy, he descended the hill to where he had left his horse, leading the animal along the bridle path which wound circuitously through the thick copse to the river road. There he mounted and walked his horse briskly behind his prisoner. Within half an hour, he had reached the ford, where a sad sight met his eyes. There had been a skirmish at this point between some British and La Fayette's rear guard. Two of the British, several of the Continental soldiers, and three horses lay dead.

On the further side of the river, when the two had crossed, the Quaker, who had slipped and fallen into the ford, stopped abruptly, refusing to advance further. He was dripping wet, and shaking as from fever.

Chapter X

HEYWARD perceived that the man was strung to the highest pitch of nervous excitement. His fear had become so great that a reaction ensued, making him well-nigh fearless in his desperation, and in a condition in which it was doubtful if he would hesitate at anything to regain his freedom. The young man armed and mounted though he was, felt that he stood in some personal danger unless he took advantage of his superior position, and he had no desire to kill or injure the man. To murder a prisoner was one thing; to deliver that prisoner safely over to honorable judgment, although death was as certain in the former as in the latter case, bore an entirely different aspect.

"Roberts," he said, leaning forward in his intense earnestness, his finger on the trigger of his musket, "unless you go quietly, I will put a bullet through your leg and let you lie here until I can ride to camp for assistance to convey you there."

For a moment it seemed as if the prisoner might fling himself at the speaker and drag him from his horse, defiant of the musket. In his mad and perhaps dying passion, should the young man fire, he would without doubt possess the almost superhuman strength of a last burst of frenzied rage, and struggle to kill his captor. But the fearless, compelling gaze, the unwavering threat of the musket cowed him. His muscles relaxed; his figure lost the intensity of its pose; his defiant expression gave way to a look of the utmost cunning and malignity. He laughed harshly and discordantly, raising one huge hand from which the water still dripped, and which trembled in his helpless rage.

"So thou wouldst drive me like cattle before thee," he cried, "with thy musket at my back and the lash of thy whip curling around my ears. Ho, ho, thou wouldst have me to hang like a gallows dog! How of the lad that will hang with me—the girl-faced brother of thy sharp-tongued Papist love?"

A startled and appalled expression passed over Heyward's face, an expression quickly controlled, but not before the Quaker had observed it.

"Yea, thou wouldst see me swinging as a spy," he mocked, "that thou and the rest of thy God-forsaken rebels might throw stones at me a-dangling with my feet off the ground. Thou and I have met before, so thou knowest I would put on no mask of hypocrisy with thee. But of the blind boy? There wouldst thou have a pretty neck to snap. Pouf! a

M

twist o' the fingers, let alone the rope.   A girl's
neck — slim and white as the Papist woman's.
Thinkest thou her tongue will not bite thee
like vinegar for this morning's work?"

Heyward passed his hand mechanically
across his eyes.   He scarcely heard the man's
words; his face had grown careworn, and he
looked white and exhausted ; the purple circles
beneath his eyes where the blood had settled
showed plainly.

"Go on," he said briefly.

In his tone was the weariness and resignation of one who has before heard the telling
of a painful thing to which he is again forced
to listen.   In the Quaker's first reference to
young Stirling, Heyward had divined the
worst.   There had been revealed to him at
once the reason for the eccentric actions he had
observed lately in Armand, and also came the
solution of his wandering out into the rain a
few nights back, and which he, his host, had
laid to somnambulism.   Whatever Roberts
should say now he knew would be but torturing repetition of that which his thought had
so instantly anticipated.

"'Tis a short tale," said the Quaker, "but
one, I reckon, which will not be o'er sweet to
thy ears.   Dost thou remember thy last day in
Philadelphia, when thou wast in the Green Tree
coffee-house with the Papist Frenchwoman?
There was I a-slumber in the corner, with an

eye half-cocked when I saw it was thou that
entered, for I suspicioned thee, friend. Dost
thou recall the letter thou lost? Yea, verily,
it was given me to see it slip from thy pocket.
Ho, ho, thou findest this not to thy liking!
Thy face grows red as a school-boy's. Yet
'twas a right sweet letter with thy cooings and
thy avowals and thy entreaties. One would
think thy soul's salvation—"

"Well," interrupted Heyward sharply.

"The blind boy's dog carried the letter to
him. Then, after thy escape from Philadelphia—for 'twas I reported thee to Lord
Howe, gathering a hint of thy position from
a word I overheard now and then when thou
wast talking with thy fine lady—'twas not
my fault, friend, thou didst not swing that
time! I bethought myself of the letter and
sought the boy. Eh, he can be seen through
as glass with his pratings of his father and of
war, and he bites at a line as a silly fish."

The sneer passed without comment. His
listener found it impossible to speak, so outraged was his sense of decency. Deep as his
contempt had been for the Quaker, it heretofore possessed no personal element. But now
the man's baneful influence cast a shadow over
that most sacred to him. The profound contempt before apparent in the young man's
glance changed to an expression of shrinking
abhorrence and active personal dislike. No

longer was he invulnerable to the maliciousness
of this creature he despised. Now was the
position of captor and prisoner an ironical
paradox, for each was at the mercy of the other.
Their eyes met understandingly for some
seconds. Then the shifty eyes of the Quaker
drooped to conceal the cunning triumph which
had flashed into them, but as he next spoke
his voice had gained a confident ring.

"Thou canst not deny the truth," he cried,
"although thou regardest me as a cur to be
spurned by thy foot. Thou seest how simple
the trick. To reseal the letter and send the
boy to return it to thee. Yea, thou eatest
thine own words, friend, and I hope the dish
relisheth thee. Thus saith the lad to me,
chuckling, ' Heyward meant not his words for
me that afternoon. But he will learn I am no
child that he talketh over my head!' Thou
seest how simple the plan. A blind boy, —
one of the Lord's afflicted, — what man sus-
picioneth him, hey? Thou shouldst know of
thine own experience how easy a thing oft falls
which seemeth difficult. 'Twas but the hoot-
ing of an owl at night. This signal the lad
would hear and follow. My bones ache yet, so
cramped was I a-waiting in the night dew, lying
low against the ground."

"How could he pass the sentry to you?"
asked Heyward, with a singular quietness of
voice that was quite distinct from the trouble

of his pale set face. He recalled an errand
which had caused him to return unexpectedly
to his quarters, to find his self-invited guest
seated writing at the table. It was the morning of the day on which Mademoiselle de
Berny arrived at the encampment. Again he
saw the fair yellow head, bright in the gloom
of the hut, moving unconsciously in unison
with the stiff painful movements of the hand
guiding the pen. He remembered that the
lad had laid down his pen and waited until
his host left the hut, the Great Dane rising
and following him to the door and then turning and going back to his master. Heyward
raised his hand imperatively, checking the answer to his question.

"I think I understand," he said slowly,
"the message was written on a piece of paper
and given to the dog who conveyed it to you.
Such a messenger the sentry would not suspect."

"Yea," said the Quaker, "the animal com-
prehends its master's wish as a human soul."
Something akin to admiration was in his cunning gaze as he perceived the quick comprehension of the plot Heyward showed, and an
added shade of insolence came into his manner, seeming to assert that it was he, and not
his captor, who had the superior position.

"How feelest thou, now, friend," he asked,
"wouldst thou now drive me into the rebels'
camp? What would thy high and mighty

Papist love say to thee? The boy is the apple of her eye, around which all her vanities centre, seeing not the Lord in her love of what is mortal."

There was a momentary silence. Heyward was looking at the man with eyes which saw him not; but Mademoiselle's face, her beautiful face, pale, agonized, formed itself in the air before him with the gaze of one mortally wounded. He heard her voice, grief-stricken, reproachful, its tone cutting his heart as a knife. He groaned, so sharp, so real was the pain.

"Thinkest thou she would speak to thee gently?" said the Quaker.

The sneer aroused the young man, recalling him to the present. He straightened himself stiffly in the saddle as one who, having had a blow, holds himself rigidly against the shock of a second. His will indomitable showed in the set lines of his face.

"Roberts," he said, in a tone absolutely unrelenting, "we will have no more words. Walk ahead of me now at a brisk pace, for we are losing time. If you refuse to do so, or attempt to escape, I will put a bullet through you."

The answering words died on the prisoner's lips, as he realized the futility of any appeal to the inexorable will which commanded him to proceed. Yet he hesitated, still defiant, al-

though once more, half-paralyzed by dread,
mumbling threats mingled with entreaties, protesting his innocence, showing himself an abject,
miserable creature, whining his late repentance
in one breath, with the next indulging in
foolish threats.

At last Heyward's self-control gave way
before the wave of passionate contempt and
loathing which surged up in his heart.

"You dog!" he cried, "do you think I
have forgotten the innocent country people
cast into prison at your bare suggestion when
you guarded the city entrances? What of our
suffering prisoners in Philadelphia, of the day
you kicked the bowl of food from a starving
soldier, of the money wrung with promise of
food — a promise you broke! And of the
boy, the boy flogged to death between you
and that devil, Cunningham! Have you forgotten — " he paused.

As swiftly as the fierce swirl of wind which
rises and dies down before the brooding storm,
so did his anger vanish almost as quickly as it
appeared. Behind his sudden gust of passion
was the mournful thought of Mademoiselle.
Well he knew that his last words were but the
cry of his conscience against the temptation to
let the Quaker go free.

"Roberts," he said, in a voice lifeless in
tone, "will you go on?" He waited with
a curious patience, as the prisoner again gave

way to another ebullition of feeling. The
man, exhausting himself at last in his rage, and
realizing his powerlessness to influence his
captor, turned with a desperate fling of his
body in the direction he was ordered to take,
and walked on. His religious training betrayed
itself now in his stress of emotion, and he
muttered broken snatches of psalms, his voice
rising at times to a monotonous sing-song.
In his fear, his reasoning power and his keener
consciousness of suffering were passive, lost
in the absorption of a fanatical condition of
mind.

That awful and desolate journey left a never-
to-be-forgotten impression on Heyward's mind.
There were less than six miles to be travelled
before Valley Forge could be reached, but to
him those miles stretched on endlessly. The
greater part of the road lay through meadows
or along the river. There was no shade to
protect them from the burning rays of the
sun. The day had developed into one of
those insufferably warm spring days which
seem more like August than May weather.

Once the Quaker, who had unconsciously
retained the chicken in his grasp, dropped
it. Heyward halted, and required him to
pick it up, taking it from him and placing
it across his saddle. The action as well as
the thought prompting it was mechanical. In
an army which had well-nigh reached starva-

tion, economy had become instinctive among
the soldiers.

The beauty of the landscape seemed a mockery to the young man : the sunny blue sky,
the green meadows, the singing of the river,
filled him with a kind of horror.   In the
Quaker's heavy drab figure plodding on
doggedly before him, and becoming confused
dizzily at times in his sight with the white
dusty road, he saw only the embodiment of
sorrow and shame he was driving into the
presence of the woman he loved.   He lost
sight of the personality of the man who, to
his tortured gaze, took on the semblance of
some huge, evil thing, which he, by a relent-
less fate, was driven to pursue, and for whose
appearance he was responsible.   He felt himself in the grasp of a temptation to resist which
was a mortal struggle.   The Quaker's evil
machinations had come to naught — the army
he sought to destroy had escaped.   To retain
him meant that Armand, also, would be arrested as a spy.   And Mademoiselle, what
justice in her suffering ?   Yet he remembered
the innocent country people cast into prison
at the mere suggestion of the man who was
now his prisoner.   He could not banish the
thought of the suffering of the American
prisoners.   Again he saw the emaciated bodies
of the ragged Continental soldiers, lying dead
at the ford he had just passed.   Their blood

called for vengeance. And as for Mademoiselle — bitterly, bitterly was he proving to her
that the soldier ranked before the lover, that
his country was more than she. But, however his heart cried out against his resolution, it was typical of the man that he
should not falter in carrying out what he believed to be his duty. With the exception of
when he had taken the chicken from the
Quaker, he had not checked his horse in its
steady gait, nor in any wise had he hesitated.
He had put his hand to the plough, and he
would not turn back, although it passed over
his happiness and that of the woman he loved.
Word by word, in torturing reminiscence, did
that eventful conversation in the coffee-house
return to him. The principles of honor and
right he had so earnestly espoused brought
forth fruit of deceit and shame. The instinct
of fear in Mademoiselle de Berny's heart,
when her brother had echoed Heyward's sentiments, had been a true one. Intuitively had
she surmised danger to the lad. In a new
light Heyward viewed his position. Not for
himself, as far as he was personally concerned,
nor for others strong enough to live by the
individual conscience, was the iron law of right
and wrong governing the masses to be kept.
But it must be kept for the sake of those
weaker human children whose feet would
stumble in following the dangerous path which

their stronger brethren passed in safety. For
Armand's actions was he largely responsible,
and Mademoiselle de Berny would most justly
consider him so. Yet now he felt that he
could see neither right nor wrong clearly, nor
did he feel that he should hesitate again, were
it necessary for him once more to enact the
rôle which his country had demanded of him
in Philadelphia. But for Diane's sake, for her
sake, his heart cried out to let the Quaker
go.

As he neared Valley Forge his feeling of
loathing and self-disgust strengthened. In his
position as it must show to Mademoiselle de
Berny there was nothing of dignity nor heroism.
Even his suffering seemed mean and ignoble,
so petty was his duty. First had she seen him
a spy, had known of his flight from Philadelphia. In thought he suffered anew from
her scorn. And now, not only must he encounter her contempt again, but he must carry
suffering and shame to her. He closed his
eyes involuntarily for a moment, his heart
sickening at the sight of the encampment
lying desolate and exposed to the glaring sun-
rays. The insignificant village of huts lay like
a blot on the smiling landscape. Squads of
men were being drilled in the surrounding
fields. On all sides were to be seen disfigur-
ing stumps of trees which had been cut down
for firewood.

He passed inside the picket line with his
prisoner, and took a road leading directly to
the guard-house, in the hope of avoiding a
chance meeting and consequent questioning of
any officer until he had imprisoned the Quaker
and had seen General Washington in reference
to young Stirling, whose unfortunate ambition
had placed him in such dangerous circumstances.
He hoped that the lad, owing to his youth and
infirmity, might be returned to Philadelphia
before any accusation could be made against
him.

But he was not permitted to convey his
prisoner quietly to the guard-house.   As he
proceeded, he saw that it would be necessary
to pass a group of soldiers who were off duty
and in whose midst he saw the fair head and
slender form of Armand.   Dreading above all
a meeting between his prisoner and his accom-
plice, he ordered the man to halt, while he
glanced around him preparatory to turning off
abruptly from the road and crossing through
a belt of scant woods.   But several of the
group had recognized the Quaker and hastened
forward.   Two of these, who were among the
first to advance, were men who had been prisoners at Philadelphia and had been exchanged.
The rest of the men followed leisurely, idly
curious as to the cause of the curses and bitter
taunts which their two comrades showered upon
the Quaker.

Heyward silenced them, however, by a sharp command. The last to approach was young Stirling, his hand on his hound's head, his face turned toward the man with whom he was walking.

He was talking and laughing gayly. His companion was the tall soldier with the vacant and foolish expression Mademoiselle de Berny had noticed the evening of her arrival at Valley Forge. This man followed the boy around with a dog-like fidelity. The two were some little way behind the rest, walking slowly down the road. The breeze blew the tattered uniform and unkempt hair of the soldier. The sunlight fell on the red heart pinned upon his broad breast. He was nodding his head as if striving to assent intelligently to the boy's words, and this effort in connection with his gentle, foolish smile was pitiable. As the two approached, the Quaker, who was surrounded by a jeering crowd, burst into a torrent of angry imprecations, his maliciousness directed toward Heyward rather than the boy whose appearance had been the touchstone to his wrath.

"Thou wouldst see another spy, hey? Seest thou his girl-face? And the dog? Yea, thou shouldst string up the animal also. Verily, it was he that fetched and carried. Another gallows-dog!" he cried with a discordant laugh, "another gallows-dog, I say!"

Young Stirling did not recognize the voice, so distorted was it by passion. He made his way swiftly through the little group with troubled face. On reaching Roberts he put out his hand and passed it over his face. Infuriated beyond reason, goaded past control by the soft and delicate touch, to a condition more animal than human, the Quaker seized the gentle hand and bit it.

His face deathly pale, Heyward, who was still mounted, brought his whip down on the fellow's head and shoulders, who put up his arms in a vain effort to ward off the blows, but was too thoroughly cowed to make any great resistance.

From the surrounding soldiers rose an angry murmur. One man, he who had been a prisoner in Philadelphia, kicked the prisoner, cursing him as he did so. Heyward seized the man by his shoulder and pushed him vigorously aside. Then he swung himself down from his horse and handed the reins to the soldier he had just reprimanded. Following the Quaker's attack young Stirling had been silent for several minutes. Suddenly he raised his wounded hand and pointed at the prisoner.

"I know you!" he cried shrilly, "I know you! I know your voice!"

Heyward commanded the men to take the reins of his horse and bind the prisoner's hands. With the exception of the quick burst

of anger the moment before, he remained the
only composed member of the group.

"Why dost thou let him go free?" cried
Roberts, as he was roughly bound. "Was't
not he that sent word to the British by me?
Is it for his girl-face and slim neck thou lettest
him alone?"

"I have no wish to go free," cried the boy
haughtily. "I am no liar to deny my act, you
dog! Neither have I a girl's face! Did you
think to force me into telling lest I should
creep out? His Excellency shall have you
whipped for your presumption, fellow," threatened the boy, with his face burning.

Dumbfounded, loath to believe his self-
accusation, doubting not that he had been
suddenly struck with madness, the soldiers exchanged astonished and pitying glances.

Heyward sought to silence the boy's shrill
talking, in the vain hope that he might protect
him from arrest for the present were he able
to get the Quaker away quietly. But Roberts
was still in a frenzy of rage and terror.

"Thou darest not let him go," he cried;
"he, too, is a spy, a spy by his own confession."

The young officer now saw no escape from
his enforced duty of putting the boy under
arrest. Still he made one last effort. Did
Armand deny the accusation, he was confident
that the Quaker's words would be counted but
malicious lies by the surrounding men. Yet

his heart sank as he saw the suspicious glances.
cast upon the boy.   There was little mercy to
be hoped for from these hard, stern men once
they learned they had been betrayed.

He commanded silence by an imperative
gesture.   His eyes challenged any disturbance
as his gaze swept the lowering, suspicious faces.
Then he turned and placed his hand on the
boy's shoulder.

"Armand," he said, in his singularly quiet
voice, "is the accusation made against you by
Roberts false?"

"No," he answered sullenly, "it was I — I
who sent a message to the British by this fellow that the rebels were going to Barren Hill."

"Then," continued Heyward, his cold glance
silencing the angry imprecations of the soldiers,
"I place you under arrest to await your trial."

The boy stood quietly while his hands were
bound.   The crazed soldier moved closely to
him.   The foolish, gentle smile was troubled.
The Great Dane, growling angrily, watched the
man tying his master's wrists, and it required
but a signal for him to spring at his throat.

"Armand," said Heyward very gently, "you
must be patient and we will try to get you out
of this.   Hand me his sword," he said, raising
his voice to address the soldier who, in com-
pliance with military discipline, had removed
all weapons from the prisoners.   Taking it,
the young officer buckled it around the owner.

The lad's heart was throbbing violently, as some prisoned bird beating itself to death against the bars; his thought was not of his being made a prisoner; he accepted the fact naturally with no comprehension of his danger. But the wound in his hand was torturing him with anger and humiliation. Until now he had never received harsh word nor blow. He felt that the shame of his injured hand was killing him. It was unspeakable degradation to him. In his agony it seemed to him that he must burst asunder the thongs confining his wrists, and throw himself on the ground. Yet he felt the hilt of his sword press against his side, and the touch comforted him. He raised his head, a light of exaltation transfigured his blind face, and his lips moved in a whisper. His expression was that of addressing some one. A great pity and gentleness came into Heyward's face.

"My dear lad," he commenced, and then turned abruptly and remounted his horse, for between his and Armand's face had risen a vision of Mademoiselle de Berny. As he was about to give the command to move on, an aide-de-camp of General Washington's rode up and handed him a message, requesting his immediate presence at headquarters. The command could not be disregarded. He knew it referred to certain knowledge he had obtained of the British tactics while in Philadelphia.

N

Reluctantly, he consigned the prisoners to
a subordinate, with a stern injunction to permit no rudeness to be passed upon them.
Then, with a last word to Armand, he wheeled
his horse around and rode towards headquarters.

Chapter XI

A LITTLE later in the morning, Mademoiselle de Berny returned with Lady Washington from a round of visits to sick soldiers. But before she ascended the stairs to her room, she went around the house to the kitchen to leave there a basket of eggs which her companion had purchased of a farmer's boy who had come into camp with eggs and fresh vegetables. As she left Lady Washington at the front entrance and turned the corner of the house, she saw Richard Heyward dismount from his horse and give it in charge of a negro attendant at the side door which opened into His Excellency's private office. She paused, half-smiling, embarrassed to advance, yet reluctant to turn back without a word from him. The young officer's eyes dwelt miserably on the charming figure in the shadow of the vine-clad wall, with its pretty affectation of domesticity, the brocaded skirt of her gown turned up from her petticoat and pinned around her waist to protect the rich material; the great basket of eggs heavy for the girlish arms. Of the wife of the Quaker preacher whose home had been made the headquarters, Mademoiselle de Berny had borrowed a poke bonnet of gray shirred cloth. Like a picture in a frame seemed her face with the ribbons tied in a bow under the chin. In her growing embarrassment beneath the young man's gaze, her face was suffused with color.

"Monsieur," she said softly, her eyes bright with laughter, despite an underlying shyness, "my basket is very heavy."

Heyward, comprehending that she had addressed him, yet in his agony of mind not taking in the sense of her words, raised his hat with a profound and abstracted bow, his only thought one of bitterness at the contrast between the bright face and the crushing blow ready to fall upon her. He opened the door of General Washington's office and went in.

Mademoiselle de Berny finished her errand to the kitchen, and ascended the stairs to her room greatly perplexed and worried. She had instinctively divined that Heyward's curious and restrained manner had not sprung from indifference nor anger towards herself, but was rather the result of some deep trouble from which he saw no hope of extricating himself. She felt that his anxious glance concerned herself, and her thought flashed to Armand with an unaccountable prescience of evil. Her heart throbbed suffocatingly. As if drawn by some curious fatality she moved restlessly to the casement of her apartment, forgetting to

remove her bonnet or unpin her gown. Down
the road which passed the house, she saw a
crowd of some thirty men, — negroes and soldiers, — and a mounted officer. The sight was
'not uncommon and she turned away. She sat
down on the little bed and began untying the
strings of her bonnet, struggling against a
desire to go in search of her brother. The
tears came to her eyes.

"Oh, Armand," she murmured, "why will
you not stay with me? Why will you not?"

Obeying an unconscious impulse, she rose
and went again to the casement. The crowd
she had discerned a few moments since had
now drawn sufficiently near for her to distinguish the faces, the recognition of some of
which overcame her with a deadly sickness, so
that she fell on her knees by the casement, her
hands clutching the sill.

She saw her brother under a guard of
soldiers, who hurried him along roughly. His
hands were tied behind him and he was bare-
headed. At his heels the Great Dane followed
growling. Striving to make his way to the
boy through the intervening men was the
crazed soldier, his tall frame overtowering
the rest. The foolish smile was gone, and in his
wild and mournful face some last intelligence
struggled for the mastery. His face was un-
dyingly stamped on Mademoiselle de Berny's
memory, as her appalled gaze passed on from

him to the huge figure at her brother's side,
and she saw the Quaker Roberts she had met
on her way to Valley Forge.

He was crying like a woman, his spectacles
all blurred with tears, so that for lack of seeing
he stumbled constantly.   But young Stirling
stepped proudly, his head held high, his face
white, save for a burning spot of color on either
cheek.   So exalted was his expression that he
seemed to be smiling.   The sunlight shone
brightly on his fair disordered hair.   On all
sides arose taunts and curses.   Owing to the
intense excitement of the early morning when
La Fayette had so narrowly escaped being
taken by the enemy at Valley Forge, an air of
restlessness still pervaded the encampment, and
a general reaction had ensued, admitting of a
certain relaxation for a time from the usual
severe military discipline.

Under these circumstances only could the
crowd have grown to be the considerable size
it now presented.   Several negroes and some
camp idlers as well as one mounted officer and
a number of other men off duty had joined the
original group of soldiers.

The guard conducting the prisoners had
turned into the very road which Heyward had
sought to avoid taking, but unfortunately, in
the young man's troubled state of mind, he
had forgotten to order otherwise.   The bitterness dormant in the hearts of the half-starved

patriots had awakened to fierce life when the
cause of the failure of the expedition to Valley
Forge became known. They had been betrayed
by spies in camp. Young Stirling turned his
head neither to the left nor to the right, as if
he heard not the jeering cries of "Spy!" nor
the curses of men whose hospitality he had
betrayed. Over the rough road he was hurried, and he slipped and fell when still several
rods from headquarters. As he half rose, his
clothing spattered with mud, a great bruise
appearing on his face, helpless to see or to use
his hands, one of the guard prodded him
with his bayonet, and a stone flung at the
Quaker missed the intended aim and struck
his shoulder, knocking him down again. Then
it was that Mademoiselle de Berny's anguish
found vent in a long and bitter cry — a cry so
exceeding bitter coming from such an unexpected direction that the guard involuntarily
turned to look for its origin.

A moment later Mademoiselle de Berny
had rushed down the stairs, out of the door,
and into the street, making her way imperi-
ously to her brother's side.

"Armand! Armand! I am here," she cried,
assisting him to rise. The Quaker, taking advantage of the momentary pause during which
attention was directed toward his fellow-pris-
oner and his sister, slipped the leathern bonds
confining his wrists. In another instant he

was struggling for his life with the guard. His expression was one to appall the stoutest heart. If the sight of her brother falling a moment since had fired Mademoiselle's heart, the scene she now witnessed froze her blood. For, although the tears were rolling down the Quaker's face, his complexion had taken on a greenish hue, and his upper lip curling back from his teeth revealed no human passion, but the ferocity of the tiger. Adding to the horror of the scene was the attitude taken by the crazed soldier, who, roused to an insane frenzy by the excitement, was engaging in the combat on the Quaker's side.

The guard, not daring to fire on account of the crowd, had resource to their bayonets. Then ensued a tragic incident. The insane soldier, his arms outstretched as if he would embrace death, flung himself violently against one bayonet, which pierced his breast. The second's hesitation of horror following the act was the Quaker's salvation. His escape, as he wrenched himself free, was so unexpected, that for a stupefied moment all were silent, watching him as he ran across the green field toward the woods like the huge, gray shadow of some evil thing fleeing the bright sunlight.

Then the crowd broke and ran, the guard leading, shouting and firing as they moved. The officer on horseback quickly distanced the other pursuers, and nearing the prisoner, checked his horse and commanded him to halt. But before the officer had time to fire, the Quaker had turned desperately and flung at him, dragged him from his horse by an almost super- human strength, and then mounted in his place, ducking to escape the rain of bullets. Another moment and he entered the cover of the woods.

Mademoiselle de Berny knelt at the side of the dead soldier, pitifully staunching the blood flowing from the wound in his breast with her handkerchief, heedless of the fact that the glazing eyes and the silent heart re- vealed the futility of her effort. She closed the eyes and crossed the helpless hands over the gaunt chest. At that moment her thought was not of herself nor of her brother, but of the mystery of life and death. Of the troops who had returned that day, all were unscathed with some few exceptions. This soldier, re- maining in camp, had met a terrible death — had been stricken down in the twinkling of an eye. Verily, the one shall be taken and the other left.

She became conscious of her brother calling her name over and over again, and, rising, she went to him and drew his shamed head down on her breast, standing with both arms around him as the soldiers closed in upon them.

How the remainder of that day and the ensuing night passed, she scarcely knew. Her

consciousness was dazed, and she felt as one
striving to awaken from a ghastly dream —
a nightmare in which the will, powerless in
the chains of sleep, cannot control the tortured imagination. She realized dimly the consideration and sympathy accorded her by
General and Lady Washington and those
other officers and their wives whom she had
met at Valley Forge. Richard Heyward she
had not seen, save the glimpse she caught of
him in the great crowd which had gathered,
following the Quaker's escape. By the next
morning she had recovered from the lethargic
condition into which the shock had thrown her.
She had risen early and dressed, and, not waiting to partake of any breakfast, had gone to her
brother. Military discipline did not permit her
to enter the building, nor to hold any communication with a spy. She was allowed, however,
to seat herself near the entrance of the guard-
house in which her brother was imprisoned.
He was sleeping on a bed of straw, the straw
partly concealed by a blanket thrown over it.
He had laid down without undressing, and his
body had the relaxed and motionless posture
of one sleeping the sleep of utter exhaustion.
One of the soldiers guarding him carried in
his breakfast, which consisted of corn bread
and coffee sweetened with molasses. He laid
it on the floor beside the prisoner, whose
heavy sleep was not to be disturbed, although

the guard spoke in rough kindness, bidding him awaken and eat.

At Mademoiselle de Berny's request the soldier took her cloak and spread it over the sleeper, who had no covering. The sober, brown hue of the garment seemed to add a tone of sadness and depression to the cheerless interior. A square of golden sunlight fell through the open doorway and cast Mademoiselle de Berny's shadow on the hard earth floor. The Great Dane lay beside his master, his head on his paws, his intelligent eyes ever watchful. Once he rose and walked over to the young girl and licked her hand with a low whine. Then he went back and lay down in his former position, raising his head to whine again as one who would proclaim that there he stationed himself a faithful watch.

Mademoiselle de Berny turned her face away and looked down the forest road, beyond the encampment to where she could see the purple sweep of far-off hills. To her wistful eyes that dreamy outline seemed to mark a fair country, where the future smiled elusively and faintly beyond the present reality.

Inside the hut the sleeper turned restlessly, drawing a long, quivering breath. After a moment he raised himself on his elbow and drew his sword from its sheath.

" Diane," he called sharply, half-awake and frowning, " what was that? "

"You are dreaming, Armand," she said.

Assured by the sound of her voice, he lay down again. She felt bitter resentment at the sight of the bruise upon his face. But for the slight movement of his chest in breathing, he seemed as one dead. His lids were transparently blue and not quite closed, as in the case of people dangerously ill. On his left cheek and temple the veins showed distinctly as some purple tracery drawn by the finger of Death. He lay now on his back, one arm outstretched stiffly, with the hand grasping his father's sword. The blade rested on the hound's back and made a line of silver light. There was an odd pathos in his attitude, as if he had dreamed of assassination and drawn his sword in fear. It was nearly an hour before he again awakened. Then he sat up on the bed and leant against the wall, flinging the cloak laid over him on the floor. He was smiling.

"Diane," he said. The habit of taking her presence for granted had become instinctive.

"Yes, dear," she said.

He turned his amused face towards her.

"We British didn't make much out of it, after all, Diane, although word was sent in time, I know. As Uncle Henry says, these rebel dogs are shrewd. Nevertheless, we served that young Frenchman a rare trick. 'Twas up the hill and down again for him."

He rose and returned his sword to its sheath, and as he did so she saw that his left hand was bound up in his handkerchief.

"Ah, Diane," he cried, with a triumphant toss of his head, "you will not laugh at me again for a little boy. It was I — I who sent word to the British. You said we were naught but bickering English, and I thought you'd be sorry for it some day."

She looked at him in dumb amazement.

He, pausing a moment for her reply, continued as she did not speak.

"I heard what you and Major Heyward said at the Green Tree coffee-house that day. You forget how I always hear things. But where are you?" he said impatiently, groping for her.

"I am here outside the doorway," she replied sadly. "They will not allow me to come in to you, Armand."

He frowned. "They'll remember this some day," he said haughtily. "But as I was saying," he continued, his face clearing as he seated himself again on his bed, and drew his hound's head against him, "as I was saying, you forgot my sharp ears that day. My father said the good God gave me my sense of hearing in place of sight."

Mademoiselle de Berny cried out bitterly, "Oh, Armand, God has punished you, inasmuch as you have used his good gift to your dishonor and mine!"

"You don't understand," he said crossly, "war is not as women think. Do you think I did not know that day when they were hunting Major Heyward that you were wondering who had told on him? I tried not to laugh when you spoke as if I knew nothing. But you can never fool me, Diane, although I am blind!"

With a cry, his listener put her hands over her face. One of the guard, his attention attracted by the sound, came over and looked in the hut, glancing sharply at Mademoiselle de Berny. But he saw nothing to confirm his suspicions, and rejoined his companions, who lounged smoking and jesting on the ground within earshot of any conversation passing between the prisoner and his sister. Mademoiselle de Berny, her face buried in her hands, had not observed the incident. Her very soul was shamed and sickened by her brother's words.

Young Stirling discovered his breakfast and commenced eating hungrily. Now and then he fed his hound pieces of the corn bread. He continued chatting to his sister. She, in her painful thought, heard his words vaguely, comprehending but dimly their significance. As she looked at him again she was startled by the impression his face conveyed to her. His profile was turned towards her, and the remarkable resemblance between them was for

the moment so great that she seemed to be
looking at herself, and not at the brother she
worshipped. Curiously enough she had no
consciousness of Armand's personality as seen
in that subtle and self-assured profile. It bore
no reference to him whatever, but expressed
her own arrogance and selfishness. It recalled
to her instantly her attitude of mind during
her last ride with General Stirling on the eventful afternoon when Heyward had betrayed his
position to her in the Green Tree coffee-house,
and she saw herself scornful of him in her own
righteousness, uttering things the reverse of
generous in her wounded love and vanity. In
contrast there rose in memory the good, honest face of her adopted uncle ; she heard his
gruff but kindly voice, uttering words which
made no impression then on her complacent
self-esteem. Now those sentences returned to
pierce her heart with shame, and she shrank
from recalling his gruff rebuke for light, vain
words, which damned ; his honest scorn of her
hinting at another's dishonor. For the first
time since her departure from Philadelphia she
thought of the anxiety General Stirling must
experience, of her lack of consideration of his
double worry in the absence of both herself
and her brother. With humiliation she remembered her outspoken desire to go in search
of her brother, her secret wish to see once more
Richard Heyward. Frank and generous was

her action on the surface, but beneath had lurked self-gratification.

Armand's voice suddenly took a pitiful, complaining tone which roused her from her reverie. He came to the doorway and held out his left hand, as if calling attention to the handkerchief which concealed a wound. Ah, how his attitude recalled those days when a little child he had turned to her when hurt, holding up his face or his tiny hand to be kissed!

"Oh, Armand," she cried, "he escaped! But you — you —"

"They will not hang me, Diane," he said quickly, comprehending her unuttered thought.

She only moaned in reply.

"They will not dare hang me," he cried, frightened and defiant. "General Washington will exchange me for one of his own men whom the British have imprisoned. Go, tell His Excellency that my father was a soldier, a soldier of the King, and that his son must not be hanged. It was not fair for Heyward to arrest me. He might have pretended he did not know. He found out from Roberts what I was doing here and he arrested me. Diane, you go and tell him to take it back. He could get me away at night without any one knowing, if His Excellency will not exchange me. I could wear his uniform, and he could give me the password."

She rose. He, hearing the rustle of her

gown, thought she was about to leave him.
He stepped quickly outside the hut and flung
his arms around her neck.

"Diane," he sobbed, "don't leave me. I
am afraid."

One of the guards came forward and was
about to separate them, but the expression of
Mademoiselle's face checked him. Full of
pain, there was an imperious entreaty in her
glance which silenced the man, so that he drew
back among his fellows with an involuntary
half-spoken apology.

"Diane," said the boy in a whisper, "send
these men away. Don't let them hang me.
Tell them that I am blind."

"Yes, yes, sweetheart," she whispered, "they
shall not hurt you. No one shall hurt you."

He pressed his cheek closer to hers, tighten-
ing his arm around her neck; his fear was
quieted immediately at her assurances.

"You will go and tell His Excellency,
Diane?" he murmured coaxingly; "yes, you
will go now, won't you? Tell him I am
blind."

She could not speak, only drawing him
closer to her. He raised his head from her
shoulder.

"Hark!" he said.

Mademoiselle de Berny and the soldiers, following the gaze of his sightless eyes as he
turned his head in the direction from which

o

the sound proceeded, saw several French soldiers lounging in front of their quarters some
distance down the road. The sound of their idle
singing arose cheerily. The words and music
were those of an old and famous chansonnette.

> " Essuyez vos beaux yeux.
> Madame de Longueville,
> Essuyez vos beaux yeux,
> Coligny se porte mieux —"

" Hark, Diane!" whispered the boy.

> " Si'l demande la vie
> Ne l'en blamez nullement
> Car c'est pour etre votre amant
> Qu'il veut vivre eternellement."

The boy's head was nodding in time to the
music. His voice rippled spontaneously into
the chorus.

> " Essuyez vos beaux yeux,
> Madame de Longueville."

One of the French soldiers made the sign
of the cross, as the language of his country
voiced in the piercingly sweet, and, for the
moment, mysterious tones came to the hearing of himself and his fellows.

"It is a voice from heaven," he said. Higher
and sweeter rang out the silvery voice.

> " Car c'est pour votre amant
> Qu'il veut vivre eternellement
> Essuyez vos beaux yeux!
> Essuyez vos beaux yeux!"

Young Stirling had dropped his arm from his sister's shoulder, and with his head flung back was singing as one who would sing his heart away. But Mademoiselle de Berny was sobbing bitterly.

Chapter XII

SOME hours later she went to General Washington, whom she found at his breakfast, served in the room which was his office. Although it was then nearly eleven o'clock, he had just risen. A glance sufficed to show that he was ill. His throat was bound by a woollen compress, and his blue military cape was wrapped closely around him, regardless of the increasing heat of the day. Doubtless it was then that the throat and lung trouble from which he died had its origin. He was studying a map which lay beside his plate. As Mademoiselle de Berny entered, he rose and, greeting her formally, handed her to a chair. Reseating himself, he pushed aside his breakfast, which she noticed was untasted with the exception of the coffee. His face was colorless. She noticed the spareness of his enormous hands, and his eyes of so colorless a gray tone as to prove his vitality to be at a very low ebb. Troubled by many thoughts, not knowing what to say first, her nature rebelling against tormenting a sick man, although the matter was one which pressed so closely upon her heart, she remained silent.

Unconsciously her companion's eyes sought

the map before him, and he made a correction
with his pencil, adding a foot-note. Then he
turned inquiringly again to his visitor. She
read in his thoughtful and attentive gaze
neither hardness to repel, nor warmth which
might give rise to hope within the breast of
a supplicant. That austere yet strangely mild
and open countenance appeared insensible to
the sway of emotions.

"Your Excellency," she said, "my brother
— he has been —" Her voice faltered.

He nodded, comprehending her unspoken
thought.

She looked away from him. Mechanically
her gaze took in every detail of the room,
with its low dark ceiling of polished rafters ;
the snowy curtains fluttering at the open casements ; the array of blue and white Delft ware
on the shelf above the chimney-hood; the
long oval table occupying nearly the whole
of the apartment, with chairs pushed in closely
together around it, now all empty and in readiness to be drawn out and occupied by Washington and his staff, meeting in consultation of
war, or when a court-martial was to be held.
So would these chairs soon be filled by men
called to pass judgment upon her brother !
It seemed to her that she had been silent a
long time. In reality, there was but a momentary pause between her first faltering words
and her next sentence.

"I do not ask justice for him, but clemency," she continued, the shamed color burning in her face. "I do not seek to excuse him, but he is my only brother."

"He is guilty of treason, my child," said Washington.

"Your Excellency, he is but a boy!"

"In my army are many lads," he answered, "who are scarcely more than children. They have suffered during the war continual privation, woe, and discouragement. Yet were one to run away and be recaptured, my painful duty would be, regardless of his youth, to have him shot as a deserter. Mademoiselle, with all my heart I should wish to be only merciful, but justice is more to be desired than kindness. My officers, as well as the common soldiers, in face of the imminent peril in which a great part of our troops stood at Barren Hill, nay, more, the peril which threatened our entire army, are hardened to clemency, and protest their right of protection against the treachery of spies. On all sides are we beset by misfortune. Not only must we struggle under an exhausting burden of debt and a worthless currency, but we must fight the foes of our own household. Mademoiselle, when we entered Boston two years ago last March, one thousand men who should have been patriots followed upon the heels of the retreating British, flying the righteous anger of their countrymen, openly declaring that if the most abject submission to us would have secured their peace, they never would have fled."

"Your Excellency," she said, with a faint and pitiful smile, "my brother was not one of those."

He did not hear her, absorbed in thought. He sat with his elbow resting on the table, his hand supporting his head. His body-servant entered and laid at his plate a small, worn journal to which there was a pencil attached by a string.

Washington did not raise his head nor seem-ingly observe the man as he carried away the breakfast things. Mademoiselle de Berny not-ing that his face was gray with pain, and that his hand was pressed against his side, half rose to go for assistance. He motioned her to re-main seated.

"In one moment I can attend to you, Mademoiselle, if you will bear with my indis-position. From my youth up I have been subject more or less to pleurisy." He drew the journal towards him, his large hand trem-bling as he jotted down with an accurate minutia of detail the private daily expenses of himself and Lady Washington. "It is aston-ishing that more fresh vegetables cannot be procured," he said, looking at her with a troubled and abstracted gaze, "and I am now paying as high as a shilling and a half for eggs."

Mademoiselle de Berny's hands gripped the arms of her chair. She felt that from nervousness she should shriek. To speak of eggs, the price of eggs, when her brother was in danger. His Excellency's face showed behind a mist of horror to her. Involuntarily she closed her eyes.

General Washington closed the journal and drew the map towards him and rolled it up. At his request his servant brought him a glass of hot toddy, and he swallowed the beverage hastily. Then he gave the map to the man with directions as to its delivery.

Mademoiselle de Berny, who had opened her eyes directly after that involuntary closing, forgot herself for the moment as she noted the ashen pallor of this great man whose supreme thought even in intensest pain was not of himself, but of his country,— that country to which he freely gave his services, accepting neither salary nor recompense.

He turned to her again, and curiously enough his next words were in answer to the tenor of her thought.

" My situation, Mademoiselle, is so irksome to me at times, that if I did not consult the public good more than my own tranquillity, I should long ere this have put everything on the cast of a die. In short, my condition is such that I have been obliged not only to use the strictest discipline, but to employ art to conceal the condition of affairs from my officers. The spirit of resigning commissions increases daily. Did I abate the severity of my discipline one jot, the soldiers would be in rebellion. I cannot afford to let them see me show mercy to one who has betrayed us."

"Your Excellency," she interposed, heart-breakingly, "he is blind!"

"Blind as he was, he worked mischief," he replied. "Mademoiselle, some of my soldiers have starved to death this winter; others will be crippled the remainder of their lives from exposure, yet would no physical infirmity pardon desertion, nor treachery on their part."

"He is all I have in the world," she said.

"Throughout the land goes up the cry of bereaved and widowed women," he rejoined.

There was a short silence. Then Mademoiselle de Berny rose as if to leave, but remained standing, her hand resting on the back of her chair. She spoke bravely, but with sinking heart.

"Once I was told, your Excellency, that your soldiers called you 'Father'; that once during a period of black despair, they crowded cheering around you. And it is repeated that you, laying your hand on the head of a drummer-boy, said: 'We may be beaten by the English, — that is the chance of war, — but here is the army they will never conquer.'"

"My child," said Washington, glancing up

at her visibly softened, "what is it you would have me do?"

"General Washington," she said, "these men who call you Father would not criticise you inasmuch as you showed mercy to the fatherless. You say no physical infirmity can pardon moral wrong. But these men who have become physically infirm through this war were once well and strong. My brother has been blind from birth. He knows not the blue sky, nor the green earth, nor the faces of those who love him. I do not seek to excuse his betrayal of the friendship shown him. But to your clemency I commend him as one unprotected and blind. I am told, Monsieur, that you have no children. Yet a country calls you Father. But I have no one in the world save him. He is but a little lad, a child in experience, too delicate to bear the weight of the punishment his deed warrants."

Washington was looking up at her, and his countenance showed him to be profoundly moved. But ere he could reply, she spoke again, no longer in a tone of entreaty nor persuasion, but with confidence and decision.

"Your Excellency," she said, "I wonder that I came to you; I wonder that I even fear your judgment, for I know absolutely that you are a humane man, and as such you could not hang him. To do so would stamp you not as a just man, but as one inhuman. Why,

Monsieur," she said, "you would not dare to do so, even if your inclination pointed that way, which you have confessed to me it did not. However the license or the discipline of military rule might sanction the deed, humanity would protest against it. Your Excellency, you dare not invoke the curse of God."

"My child," said Washington, with great gentleness, "rest assured that—"

"General Washington," she interrupted, "not only as his sister, but in the name of those of my country-women who have so generously given their sons to your cause, I ask that you be equally generous and give me the life of my brother whose mother was a Frenchwoman!"

"Mademoiselle de Berny," he said, "believe me that your appeal touches my heart; but, until I have given the matter further thought, I cannot reply to you. Rest assured, however, that not only is your brother in my hands, but he is in the hands of God. There is one question now which it is my painful duty to ask you. I beg you will be seated."

She sat down in the chair from which she had risen, leaning forward in her anxiety as to what he would have to say. Washington glanced away from the intent and questioning gaze of those eyes, so clear and open that one seemed to look down into the honorable and proud heart of the owner, with the reluctance of meeting the look of pain which he was aware his next words would bring. But he forced himself to meet her gaze, speaking deliberately and coldly.

"Mademoiselle de Berny, since your brother's arrest it has been suggested to me by my own thought, as well as by several of my officers, that the question would arise, nay more, it has arisen, whether or not you had anything to do or any previous knowledge of your brother's actions. It becomes my painful duty to inform you, that since his arrest you have had, as far as appearances went, perfect freedom. On the contrary, you have been under the constant secret surveillance of a guard, who are instructed to permit you such liberty as is compatible with your being kept a prisoner here at Valley Forge."

As a bird, fascinated, powerless to remove its gaze from the enemy, Mademoiselle de Berny was staring helplessly at him.

"I have stated this," continued Washington, "in order that I might ask one question of you, which, if answered to my satisfaction, will remove suspicion from you, and I will take upon myself the responsibility of your future bearing here. Were you aware until his arrest of any of your brother's plans or desire to betray us to the British?"

But the girl in front of him could not speak. As the Quaker's attack upon her brother had well-nigh crushed the boy, so now the sister's bright nature was broken. She had been surrounded and under guard as a common spy! She strove to speak, but no sound issued from her parched lips. Again and again her lips moved in a vain effort, until at last her half-paralyzed will asserted itself, and she voiced in a whisper her denial. But as that half-truth faintly whispered left her pale lips, something else passed from Mademoiselle de Berny's life. Never again would she have the same lightness and same free-heartedness and buoyant self-confidence. With that supreme effort at denial, something which was vital in her nature was killed. Tenderer for this experience she would always be, but her pride was gone. Perhaps something of this made itself felt to Washington, and that in her gaze he read something of that look which it is said the dying deer turns upon the hunter who has slain it. He bent to catch her whispered words which he could scarcely distinguish. Only now, as in his first interview with Mademoiselle de Berny, he saw again a fleeting resemblance in her face to that of a long-past love of his, "the Lowland Beauty," the unrequited love of his youth. The quivering of this French girl's sweet mouth, with its full and girlish curves, brought to him again the memory of one unkissed mouth; the slender hands pressed together were like that pair of hands which had slipped

from his eager grasp; hair as soft and shining
had shadowed other eyes, eyes which had
turned from him. Oh, the distant and en-
chanting glory of youth! He covered his
eyes with his hand. He was not a military
genius, but he was a great soldier; but before
that he was a peace-loving man, and his
thought turned wearily from the smoke and
din of battle to the quiet and beauty of the
country. This young girl had spoken of the
fact that he had no children, but that a country termed him Father. Yet there was the
personal part of his nature, which cried out
for a child of his own flesh and blood. In
his expression was an elusive sadness, a profound melancholy indicative of a nature whose
generous sentiments had been misunderstood.
The jealousy and treachery of some of his
officers, the lack of sympathy shown him by
Congress, had chilled a nature naturally reserved and self-contained. His face, showing
much patience and power of endurance, nevertheless bespoke a weariness verging upon exhaustion, as one who had received ingratitude
from those he served and had found glory a
vanity. He removed his hand from his eyes
and addressed his companion.

"Mademoiselle de Berny," he said, "I am
convinced of your innocence in this matter. I
trust you will do me the justice to believe that,
painful as the question I asked must have been

to you, it was equally painful to me to put a
seeming affront upon one who is not only my
guest and of the French people, but one who
is a woman as well and doubly entitled to consideration."

Mademoiselle de Berny rose, but remained
standing a moment.

" Your Excellency," she said bravely, "what
of my brother?"

A coldness and austerity which appalled her
made itself felt in Washington's manner. His
stern glance frightened her, making her grow
faint from dread, lest in her last question she
had overstepped the bounds of his patience,
and had undone all that she had just accomplished. He rose and laid his heavy hand
upon her shoulder. His figure more imposing by reason of the military cape, his majestic,
dome-like head made him an overpowering
personality in the small room, which was a
dwarfed and meagre setting for this great man.

" My child," he said, " you have had what
assurance I am able to give you, until a proper
consultation with my officers is held."

Mademoiselle de Berny made no reply.
The hand laid upon her shoulder was to her
tortured heart a cruel weight with power to
crush. Near her was the door leading into
the hall.

" Remember," said His Excellency kindly,
" that aside from this Lady Washington and I

will be honored to grant you any favor within our power."

She did not speak, her eyes were fixed upon the hall door, which opened a blessed avenue of escape when that heavy hand should be lifted from her shoulder.

With an irrepressible sigh, as he divined her feelings, Washington's hand dropped to his side.

"Mademoiselle de Berny," he said, "I am about to review the troops, and I shall leave this room at your disposal, where, if you desire, you may rest until you feel better able to return to your brother. I would urge my advice in this instance as you appear to be physically exhausted."

He opened the drawer of the table and placed within the papers and maps he had been correcting and locked the drawer, putting the key in his pocket. His great exactness showed itself in the careful placing of these papers; in the particular unvarying position of the ink-well, quill-pen, and blank paper in the centre of the table. From the chimney-shelf he took his hat and riding-whip, which he uniformly laid there. Then, without further word to the young girl, who had again seated herself, he opened the door and went out, closing it behind him.

Mademoiselle de Berny shivered at the sound, and her hands clasped convulsively.

At last she was alone! Her bosom rose and fell quickly from her tumultuous breathing. She was like a bird which had escaped from the snare of the fowler — a bird uncaptured, but fluttering with a broken wing. With the closing of the door between herself and Washington had come a blessed relief — release from pain. All that ideal sentiment she had held sacred had been violated, and the last blow had come from Washington. As a rough touch leaves an ineffaceable mark upon the petals of a flower, so his statement, that she had been virtually a prisoner under suspicion as a common spy, had bruised a nature so highly strung and of such delicacy that a false accusation cast upon it fell as a wound and not as an insult, rendering the receiver incapable of resentment.

For a little while His Excellency ceased to signify a great and humane man to Mademoiselle de Berny. His words had invested him with a kind of horror, so that she shrank from the memory of him as one loathing the instrument which had dealt a wound. With closed eyes she prayed she might never look upon his face again. She thought of Richard Heyward, and somewhat of relief came into her expression. She opened her eyes and the room was magically changed. True, there were the same snowy curtains fluttering at the casement; as brightly blue as before was the array of blue and white china on the chimney-shelf; there was the long table with the empty chairs pushed in around it; above her head there still remained the low, dark ceiling with its polished rafters. But the horror of the room was gone, gone with that colossal figure which had made it a small, mean place.

With the absence of that sad, austere, and yet benevolent countenance the room lost its air of a justice court, and recovered a certain sweet simplicity, as of a domestic life passed within its walls, breathing peace and comfort. As a golden sunlight penetrating a gray and melancholy mist, so now the atmosphere of the room lately thick with horror and shame — so that she felt as if every breath of air suffocated her — steadily brightened beneath the beneficent thought of her lover. He it had been who had first violated those Old World sentiments of honor, becoming gentle people among whom she had been born and bred, but now at the last it was he who restored serenity to her troubled soul. It consoled her deeply to remember he had abided, to the bitter end, by the principles in which he believed. With the unerring instinct of love she comprehended what remorse his must have been when he arrested her brother. Although her own heart were sacrificed in the struggle, it counted as nothing beside the fact that he had stood loyal. Now, amid her shattered ideals and outraged

sentiments, her brother's shame and the blighting suspicion cast upon herself, the thought of
Heyward was as an oasis in the desolate wastes
of her happiness. The little room was dim
behind a mist of tears.

Chapter XIII

YOUNG Stirling, recommended to the mercy of the court, did not receive the penalty his crime warranted, but was sentenced to imprisonment as an unsafe person until such time as he could be returned to his guardian, General Stirling, of His Majesty's Army. Although he had been openly convicted as a spy, he was treated indulgently by the officers and soldiers over whom he exercised an irresistible charm. His gay humor, his haughty and self-consequential bearing, his fragile beauty and his incurable blindness, the devotion of the great hound to him and, above all, perhaps, his mourning attire and the sword of his soldier-father, which he wore with such importance, touched that which was best and tenderest in the roughest as well as the most discouraged men.

But of all this consideration shown him, which would have so gratified her loving pride, had she known it, Mademoiselle de Berny was unconscious. The day following her interview with General Washington she had spent with her brother in the guard-house, and late in the afternoon, feeling utterly wearied, she had returned to headquarters to rest for a short while. She climbed the narrow, little stairway leading to

her room and lay down on her bed; that bed
from which she did not rise for nearly three
weeks, and which it appeared for a time she
never would leave again, worn out by the
anxious strain and exposure to which she had
been subjected.

During those days when her illness seemed
liable to terminate fatally, her brother, granted
permission by Washington, stationed himself
in a corner of the bedroom with his faithful
hound beside him. And often in the watches
of the night, when the girl tossed and moaned
in delirium, he would play gently on his flute,
sometimes singing little folk-songs in his
mother's tongue, which were like airs of sunny
France blowing softly in the sick-room, so that
at last the patient grew quiet and soothed.
But he refused with strange and even angry
insistence to leave his corner and move nearer
the bed. Not once did he approach his sister.
Only the Great Dane, standing as high as the
small bed, would draw near and lick the little
fevered hands, whining pitifully until spoken
to reassuringly by the nurse, a colored woman
belonging to Lady Washington.

As Mademoiselle de Berny grew better, her
brother spent less and less of his time with her,
slipping out of the room at the first opportunity
and back to the guard-house, where he was
virtually imprisoned, there to pass long idle
hours talking and jesting with the soldiers;

practising with his sword, fencing with remarkable skill, blind as he was, as though possessed
by a sixth sense to locate his opponent and
gauge his movements. His chief delight, however, was to seat himself upon the great stump
of an old oak tree, which had been hewn down
just outside the guard-house door, and there
lead the men in song.

He played a fiddle he had purchased of a
negro, giving in exchange one of his jewelled
knee-buckles.

Several days prior to the breaking up of
camp, General Washington, passing by the
guard-house on his return from a review of his
troops, checked his horse to listen to the music.
Lulled by the languor of the warm June day, a
number of soldiers lounged on the ground in the
shade of the trees, smoking and jesting or joining in the singing. As Washington drew up
his horse, the jingle of "Yankee Doodle" rose
lustily. His Excellency motioned the men to
continue, and remained listening, his white horse
pawing the ground; his gaunt face was pleased,
although unsmiling, as his gaze rested benignly
on his men. As the song ended and he was
about to ride on, the fiddle continued playing
without a break in the time. The tune was
the same, but Armand's voice rose to different
words, which were at once recognized by his
companions. The song now was a parody
made by some British wag upon the Continental

air of "Yankee Doodle," and greatly in vogue
the past winter in Philadelphia.

> "When Congress sent great Washington,
> All clothed in power and breeches,
> To meet old Britain's war-like sons,
> And make some rebel speeches,"

There was a murmur from the men. Their
eyes sought the impassive countenance of their
commander. He raised his hand, enjoining
silence on their part. In his deep eyes lurked
a still humor. The prisoner sat perched upon
the stump, one leg doubled under him, his
foot tapping his hound's back. His fair hair
gleamed pale gold in the sunlight; his face
was afire with daring and laughter. Only his
eyes were blank and staring.

> "'Twas then he took his gloomy way,
> Astride his dappled donkey's,
> And travelled fast both day and night,
> Until he reached the Yankees.

> "Full many a child came into camp,
> All clad in homespun kersey,
> To see the greatest rebel scamp,
> That ever crossed o'er Jersey,"

Sang the laughter-thrilling voice, ringing out
with mocking sweetness. The effect was irresistible. From sheer spontaneity the men broke
into a murmur of the tune.

"The rebel clowns ! Oh, what a sight !
  Too awkward was their figure.
'Twas yonder stood a pious wight,
  And here and there a nigger !

"The patriot brave, the patriot fair,
  From fervor had grown thinner,
So off they marched with patriot zeal
  And took a patriot dinner."

On His Excellency's face was a rare smile. There is the responsibility of the individual soldier ; there is a greater responsibility of the commander. And sometimes it happens to one in authority that he is made to feel the burden of his liability as something greater than can be borne, so that his own personality becomes an irksome thing to him, inasmuch as he can no longer regard himself lightly nor inconsequentially. A mere song had accomplished much, so that for a little while Washington lost his seriousness in his own eyes, and the heavy cloak of tormenting care seemed to have slipped from his shoulders. So oftentimes does a jest cheer the heart and invite hope. But there was something of the pedagogue in Washington which would not permit him to let the prisoner's action pass unreproved. He guided his horse nearer the group, raising his hand to enjoin silence among the men. He perceived that the boy was about to speak, and he awaited his words with some curiosity and amusement.

Young Stirling, having finished singing, laid
the fiddle down on the ground beside him.
Then with the manner of a man having a good
story to tell, a manner so evidently imitative
and confident as to be absurd in one so boyish,
he crossed one leg indolently over the other
and clasped his hands around his knee. He
turned his head from side to side, listening a
moment.   Then he laughed mischievously.

" Methinks you fail to find that jingle ring
sweetly, friends.   Yet the tune was the same
as your own 'Yankee Doodle.'   Perhaps you
liked not the reference to your 'patriot dinner.' I wonder not that continual fare of hasty
puddin' and molasses has made you a trifle
thin-skinned and sensitive to the mention of
it.   Even during my short stay here my
stomach has grown aweary of it," he paused,
laughing, but resumed talking in another moment.

" I was about to tell you a tale — a rare
good tale, my father used to say. Many a
time has he brought his hand down smartly
on his leg — so — and taken his pipe from
his mouth to laugh at the thought of it.
' By the Lord Harry,' he would say, shaking
his head, 'like music!' and he would fall to
chuckling again over it."

The speaker grew silent, leaning a little
forward, his face lit by a dreamy smile.

" He loved a good joke so," he said softly,

speaking to himself with a musing nod.   Suddenly recollecting the present, he drew himself up again and continued his story.

"'Twas in the Seven Years' War, and His Excellency, General Washington, was then a good Tory.   It seems, so my father said, that His Excellency wrote an account of a skirmish with the French at Great Meadows, in which he beat them because of his English blood, and sent the tale to England where it was printed.   And in the account he wrote that the 'whistling of bullets was like music!' 'Tis said King George's face was worth running for to see when he read it.   'For,' said His Majesty, shaking with merriment, 'if he had heard more, he would not have thought so!'"

Washington's mouth twitched.

"If I did use that phrase, sir," he said in a low and amused tone, "it must have been when I was very young."

The prisoner, confounded by the unexpected retort, started to his feet.

"Your Excellency!" he cried.

"I must ask you, young sir," continued Washington, in his peculiarly low and constrained yet penetrating voice, "if you consider it becoming a gentleman that in your present circumstances you sing unseemly songs, and indulge in jesting at the expense of one who has befriended you?"

The boy's bright face grew sullen and the eyelids, dropped over the sightless eyes, quivered.

It was characteristic of Washington that, following a just reprimand, the great benevolence of his nature warmed his austere manner as sunlight a wintry landscape. He looked down at the desolate, boyish figure in its black garments, and saw the sullen, defiant pride in the set face.

"My lad," he said kindly, "I am told that your father met a brave death on the field, and was a man of excellent parts. Think you that he would consider his son had shown either courage or the well-breeding of a gentleman could he see him now? I have no doubt that you hoped to benefit your King, but you must remember, young sir, that, although your desire was honest, in fulfilling it you betrayed the hospitality shown you by your enemy, and also acted without military authority from the side you hoped to benefit."

The prisoner made no reply. In the silence that followed, His Excellency turned his horse and rode away. Young Stirling remained standing until he no longer heard the hoof-beats of Washington's horse. Then, with white face and without a word, he turned and entered the guard-house. He seated himself on his bed, speaking seldom to any one, refusing food brought him, arrogantly. But in the

darkness and silence of the night, his pride
vanished and he lay weeping, choking back
his sobs that the sleeping soldiers might not
hear him, his restless, wakeful head buried
in his straw pillow, his face hot and wet with
tears, with one arm outstretched and clasped
convulsively around the neck of his dog.

When morning came, he would neither rise
nor lift his head from the pillow, lying motionless and silent, and ignoring the food laid beside him.   All day he lay so.   But towards
six o'clock he rose and availed himself of the
permission which had been accorded him to
visit his sister.   He called to his hound, and
passed the guards without a word, his manner
haughty and repellent.   One of the guard followed him, but turned back satisfied when he
saw the boy enter headquarters.

Mademoiselle de Berny's room was empty
of any attendant.   Young Stirling passed in
noiselessly and seated himself in his customary
corner.   The mellow light of the early evening came in through the single open casement
of the primitive room with its spotless sanded
floor and its homely furniture.   On the case-
ment-sill a broken-mouthed pitcher held a
branch of the thorny wild yellow rose; the
air was filled with the fragrance of the blossoms.   At one end of the room was a row of
nails for clothing, and there the young girl's
dress was hung—a mass of soft primrose

color in the delicate light. In the narrow little bed, whose white draperies had been removed, and which had been drawn out into the centre of the room, Mademoiselle de Berny was sleeping sweetly. She lay on one side of the bed, the braid of her hair and one arm hanging over the edge, the slender fingers — a little pink with returning health — nearly touching the floor. Shortly after her brother's entrance she awakened.

"Armand," she said, not seeing him but conscious of his presence.

"I am here," he answered.

They were the first words exchanged between them since her illness.

"Come here, dear," she said.

He remained motionless. She raised herself up in bed. In the fading light she saw him in the further corner of her room, the massive head of the Great Dane clasped closely to his breast. His face was turned towards her, and she saw it wan and of an almost transparent whiteness, and his eyes were wide open and staring. As in the eyes of the hound she had often perceived an intelligence which seemed struggling for expression, so now in the lad's sightless eyes Mademoiselle de Berny felt the mind behind striving to shine through the blankness — to pierce the light of day.

"My darling," she cried, putting out her arms to him, "what is it?"

The miserable set look of his countenance underwent no change as he answered her.

"He spoke as if I were a child," he said dully, "and he told me my father would be ashamed of me."

"Oh, Armand," she interrupted pitifully, "who has been talking to you?"

"Last night I heard two of the soldiers talking about it too," he continued in the same listless tone. "They said I did not know any better — that I was only a boy and a tool of Roberts. They said that, Diane, when it was I, I who sent word to the British that the Marquis de La Fayette was going to Barren Hill," his voice rose shrilly, "yet these rebels might have been ruined through me had the Quaker made better time with the message. They lied! They lied, Diane, when they said I did not know any better."

"Armand," pleaded Mademoiselle de Berny, deeply troubled, "won't you tell me who has been talking to you?"

"It was General Washington," he answered. "He said I had no right to be a spy. Yet he sent Major Heyward to Philadelphia, Diane, to find out things for him. Then why should he say I did wrong and not his own soldier?"

"Because," she answered gravely, "Major Heyward was sent there by his commander, and you acted without military authority. Moreover, while he was not thinking of

himself, but only of serving his country in becoming a spy, you thought of your own glory.
Wasn't it so, Armand?"

"Yes," he whispered. After a little he began
to cry, his face pressed against his dog's head.

"I wanted my father to know," he said; "I
wanted him to know."

"Won't you come to me, dear," said Mademoiselle de Berny, her own eyes wet with tears,
her loving arms extended.

"I am coming," he said brokenly, and rose.
Half-way across the room to her he paused and
then went on. That momentary hesitation was
the last resistance his pride made against the humiliation fallen upon him. Mortification at his
sister's reproval and condemnation of his action,
when he was first imprisoned, had filled him
with resentment so bitter that he would not approach her during her illness. Now a keener
mortification drove him to hide his shamed face
upon that tender breast from which in his
wounded self-love he had turned.

He seated himself on the bed beside her, and
she drew his head down on her shoulder as she
sat propped up by her pillows.

"I wish my father were here," he whispered;
"we always got along together. We were such
good fellows together."

"I know," she answered tenderly, holding
him closer.

He moved restlessly and lifted his head. His

expression had changed magically and was full
of eagerness and excitement. His voice rang
confident and strong.

"We used to talk about it," he cried, "when
I should go to camp with him. And if there
were a battle, I was to ride close beside him with
a musket and a sword."

He flung his arms out wildly.

"There would be the smoke thick around
us, and the music and the shouting and firing.
And we two would know we were there together,
fighting side by side and — and," his voice trembled and died down, and his head sought its
resting-place once more on her shoulder. His
thin arms went round her neck in a tight
embrace, his cheek was pressed against hers.
Ill as Mademoiselle de Berny had been, the fire
of life burned faintly in her cheeks and mouth
and shone in her eyes which were brooding and
tender as a mother's. But the lad's eyes were
closed and his lips were pale. Seen thus in the
twilight one face might have been taken for the
death masque of the living, so marvellous was
the resemblance.

Though Mademoiselle de Berny comprehended her brother's loneliness for his father,
and wondered at the circumstances which had
recently arisen to grieve him, her thought was
mostly passive in these moments of blissful
nearness. That love which possesses the
maternal element asks little and questions not

if only the one beloved is near. And Mademoiselle's affection for her brother was satisfied to hold him safely in her arms, supremely confident that there neither sorrow nor harm might touch him. When the colored nurse entered the room with a tray on which was placed her patient's supper and two lighted candles, Mademoiselle de Berny raised her free hand warningly.

"Hush," she whispered, "he is asleep."

At the further side of the bed the Great Dane's head appeared as he raised himself up from his position on the floor to growl at the intruder.

Q

Chapter XIV

A WEEK later, on the sixteenth of June, at the break of day, a messenger rode post-haste into the camp at Valley Forge with the information that the British had evacuated Philadelphia the preceding day and crossed the Delaware. So quietly did they leave that many of the citizens became aware of their departure only by the absence of the red-coats in the street.

"They did not go away," wrote a resident, "they vanished."

And this same messenger brought rarely good tales of the action of those loyalists left in the city, how they besieged the British with entreaties to leave a guard in Philadelphia to protect them from the rebels; how neither money nor entreaties had had effect with the red-coats, who roughly retorted that the frightened peace lovers should have thought of the future before; how over three thousand miserable loyalists had fled into the country or crossed the Delaware, following upon the heels of the British Army.

With the exception of the wife and daughter of the Quaker preacher, whose home had been made the headquarters, Mademoiselle de Berny was the only woman in camp. Lady Washington and other of the wives of the officers had left for their homes fully a week ago, their departure being deemed expedient even then, for it was not known what day the army might break camp.

From her casement Mademoiselle de Berny watched the activity and bustle going on in the camp ; heard the ringing commands of the officers ; saw the prompt obedience of the soldiers, for both officers and men were cheered and quickened into new life at the prospect of action after the long and weary waiting. But to Mademoiselle de Berny, as yet not sufficiently recovered to bear much change, the sight was stamped with melancholy. She leaned a little out of the casement, looking down on the busy scene with its masses of moving men and horses ; of troops forming in the fields ; from the chimneys of the huts rose the blue smoke curling in the sunlight, as the men hastily prepared a dinner before starting ; groups of soldiers were washing at the river brink and filling their canteens.

Beyond the river on the long hill slope slept the dead ! There they lay at rest. Their weary march was over, their bowed and burdened heads resting on the bosom of the earth, as their souls rested in God. Defeated in the struggle with famine and cold, they had lain down in uncertainty as to whether their cause

would win or not.   Between them and their
comrades the grass grew soft and green.   Did
they know, slumbering sweetly, that soon they
would be left alone, lying buried row on row,
adown the hill slope, their faces turned to the
east whence the sun should rise?   Perchance
their good right hands still clasped their mus-
kets, as if at the word of command they would
arise — a mystic host, to defend the deserted
encampment at Valley Forge.   In the young
girl's heart was an indefinable yearning which
sprang from her physical exhaustion and the
trials she had undergone, to drop behind from
the quick on-marching ranks of the living and
slip away from them back to the quiet resting-
place of the dead.   And she knew not that
this desire was a homesickness, a longing for
the happy past which was forever put away
from her.   Against her future as she then conceived it to be, she rebelled as a sick and
lonely little child, fighting the terror of darkness in the night.   She turned her head away
from the casement and closed her eyes.   She
had shared the common fate of those who
had entered Valley Forge.   She had reached
the encampment with the color of the rose in
her face and with a light heart.   She would
leave it in a few hours tried to the soul, and
with a face wan and pale as the waxen snow-
drops which pushed their frail way through the
dead leaves of the past fall.

By the late afternoon the main body of the
army had formed in marching order, and was
moving rapidly toward the Delaware in pursuit
of the British. It was sometime later before
the detachment Washington left in charge of
General Benedict Arnold, — whose arm recently
injured rendered him unfit for active duty, — to
proceed to Philadelphia and hold the city, was
able to start. This division numbered all the
infirm and disabled.

It had been decided that Mademoiselle de
Berny should not go unaccompanied by any
woman, as the ride was a long one and to be
taken at night. So the wife of the preacher,
Isaac Potts, a good and motherly Quakeress,
who had conceived a very kindly liking for her
guest, had been requested by His Excellency,
General Washington, to see that Mademoiselle
reached Philadelphia safely, where she would
doubtless find friends, although her guardian,
General Stirling, had, in all probability, departed
from the city with the British Army.

Moreover the good woman was glad of the
opportunity thus afforded her to make a visit,
long deferred by the war, to some relatives in
Philadelphia, and it was with great bustling and
chatter that she prepared for the journey, which
she was to take on horseback, seated on a pillion
behind a soldier. Mademoiselle de Berny,
wrapped in the long brown cloak in which she
had come to Valley Forge, was lifted by Isaac

Potts in front of Major Heyward upon his horse. She was still very weak, and it being neither safe to permit her to ride alone nor on a pillion, the offer of the young man to take charge of her on the ride had been accepted by the shrewd and kindly Quakeress, who had guessed at the condition of affairs between the two young people, and whose heart had warmed toward the young officer during the period of Mademoiselle's illness. Many mornings had his tall figure darkened her kitchen door, and his spurred boots left muddy tracks upon the dazzling whiteness of her floor as he entered and seated himself near the table at which she was cooking, his sombre face brightening beneath the magic of her cheerful presence and her assured and hopeful statement that the health of Mademoiselle was improving.

The young girl was amazed and disconcerted by the position in which she found herself. She had believed Richard Heyward to have left with the main troops earlier in the day, and had not the least suspicion that the officer who was to be her escort would prove to be he. She greeted him with shaken composure, too greatly embarrassed to trust herself to speak. She turned her head aside, leaning slightly forward, her hands fastened for support in the horse's mane.

The troops were already started and had been gone some few moments. Young Stirling had

gone with them; in his eagerness to keep with
the men he had not waited for his sister. The
Quakeress, who had caused the slight delay in
the little party, was hastily assisted by her husband to the pillion behind the soldier who was
mounted and waiting impatiently for her. As
soon as she was safely settled, he chirruped to
his horse, passing on some distance ahead of
Major Heyward, who had dismounted to tighten
the girth of the animal he rode. The comfort-
able, amply proportioned figure of the Quakeress shook with every jolt. Her bonnet, shaped
like a scoop, was tied securely under her chin,
framing a face wholesome and fair, although
much wrinkled, as a winter apple is still red and
sound and sweet, despite its withered skin. Her
feet shod in low, broad-toed shoes, her substantial ankles betraying white hosiery, swung against
the horse's side. On her lap she held a basket
of eggs and berries and a bouquet of homely
garden flowers, a gay and fresh bit of color.

Mademoiselle de Berny glanced from the
Quakeress' vanishing figure back to the house
they were leaving — that house but a few hours
since the headquarters of an army. Now it
seemed to have regained magically the serene
atmosphere of a Quaker preacher's home. The
green sweeping boughs of the trees overshad-
owed its low stone walls. The honeysuckle
and roses were in bloom around the tiny verandah. In the back yard a negress was hang-

ing out the wash and singing. She saw the
casement swinging in the breeze and the fluttering of the white curtain in the little room
which had been hers. Nevermore would she
be there! Isaac Potts waved his hand in farewell, and although she smiled in response, the
little black figure of the preacher standing in
his doorway was obscured by a mist of tears.
She was conscious that Major Heyward mounted
behind her and started the horse, but she kept
her face turned from him, remaining silent in
her deep embarrassment — an embarrassment
which was reflected in her companion. He
had offered his services to the Quakeress as
an escort to the young girl left in her care,
knowing that Mademoiselle de Berny knew
none of the other officers in the division en
route to Philadelphia, and having also a natural desire that she should not be put in charge
of a common soldier. Now he doubted if his
solicitude had been wise, as he noticed the
nervous color fluttering in her pale cheek
turned from him; the rigid lines of the slender figure held as far forward and away from
him as possible. He felt the violent protest
of her whole nature against the position in
which she was placed, and realized sadly how
very ill she must have been, how weak she
still was that this protest was passive and took
no active form. Her high spirits, her old daring and laughter, were gone.

Now she shrank from him, showing plainly that the memory of their misunderstanding still rankled in her breast. He bitterly regretted that she had not been put in a stranger's care rather than in his, as in her present nervous condition he served only to terrify her. His lack of forethought acquired a criminal aspect to him as he observed the tense grasp of the little hands fastened for support in the horse's mane; the frail figure holding itself in such proud reserve, a reserve which must soon give way at the demands of exhausted nature and force her to claim his arm — that arm from which she shrank — as a support. His right arm hung free at his side, ready to catch her should she slip. With his left hand he held the reins.

The air was filled with the ineffable brightness and mellowness of a spring day drawing serenely to its close. The river, reflecting the sunset, ran smoothly save where its glassy surface broke into a myriad of golden ripples as the horses crossed the ford. The breeze, soon to become chilly when no longer warmed by the sun, was already freshening, imparting new life to the troops, which numbered many sick and half-invalid members to whom the day had been almost insufferably warm. The golden rays were withdrawn first from the woods so cool and green that as the men passed within its shade twilight seemed to have closed in upon them.

Through the slight delay at starting, Major Heyward and his companion were in the rear of even the last stragglers of the troops who marched pretty much as they pleased upon this occasion.   Even the soldier behind whom was mounted the Quakeress kept well ahead of the two.   Now and then, for the highway had many curves, they caught a glimpse at a turn of the road of the Quakeress' solid drab figure, little disturbed by the jolting of the horse.   The gay tints of the nosegay she carried appeared like some great variegated flower against the surrounding greenness.   But there were times in which even the good woman's figure disappeared beyond a curve for so great a length of time that Mademoiselle de Berny and her escort seemed entirely alone in the forest with the exception of several Indians, followers of the camp, walking behind.

There had been but little conversation between the two, and then the few remarks made had been desultory and impersonal.   Both felt as if they were moving in a dream, and had little consciousness of time beyond a bitter anticipation of the parting moments drawing steadily nearer as they approached Philadelphia, where they would separate in uncertainty as to whether they would ever meet again.   The girl's heart was filled with jealous pain, and before her mental gaze the possible future unfolded. There would be one brief moment of farewell, a slight clasping of the hands, and then they would go their separate ways — she back to France and he — ah, he would remain in this young country to forget his one-time love for her, for a woman who had been reared to the same ideals as he, until even his memory of his former fancy grew confused and her personality became merged into that Old World society whose sentiment he despised, whose honor was strained in his estimation, and whose customs he scorned. Ah, well, she had learned her lesson. Those weeks at Valley Forge had revealed a moral breadth and noble simplicity of life, which, although she longed for it, she felt was not for her. It was too high an altitude. More freely could she breathe in the vitiated and artificial air of the court; there were the surroundings most suitable to her development. A scion of old France, she would be drawn back again to her own people as Heyward would be to his. But had it been different! Little could Mademoiselle de Berny foresee the revolution impending in her country, a revolution so terrible that it could have been born only of the two extremes, — a pampered and effete nobility and a starving people. She would escape no more in France than America those questions which were troubling her now, and had perplexed her sorely at Valley Forge.

Richard Heyward looked down anxiously at her, wondering at her prolonged silence which chilled him, depriving him of courage to speak. In the western sky, seen faintly rose-colored through the trees, the evening star brightened silverly. Mademoiselle de Berny's hair escaping from the confinement of her hood was blown softly about her face. Against his coat lay one tress like finely spun silk. His thought reverted to his old comparison of her hair to the reddish bronze of oak leaves in sunshine. Only now in the dimness there was no gleam in her hair, but it was the color of a dead leaf, brown and curling, blown against his breast. His gaze dwelt hungrily on her leaning forward as far as possible from him, her head turned so that he could see but her profile, subtle, reserved, beautiful, shadowed by the brown hood of her cloak and the softly moving curls of her hair. At times her loveliness aroused a curious emotion in him, affecting him painfully, so little candor it revealed, so little to be possessed did it seem. A certain hopelessness would arise within him so that in her presence was he most lonely, most remote from her.

She, striving to push the rebellious locks back beneath her hood and being still very weak, commenced trembling in her embarrassment. Fearing she was chilled he checked the horse and removed his coat, placing it around her shoulders, at which action she protested, striving ineffectually to put the garment from her. In removing his coat he appeared in his ruffled shirt, the whiteness of which made more distinct the darkness of his face. Her glance fell upon his hand. In his anxiety lest she should fall he had passed this arm lightly around her. It rested against her cloak, its strength refined by the overhanging ruffle — a hand delicate and finely formed, expressing a nervous intensity indicative of the man. Now, in Mademoiselle de Berny there grew a great humbleness, so that had it been possible she would fain have bent and laid her face against his hand, quite content if life, which had grown so bitter, might slip from her, remaining thus very quietly with hidden face.

"Monsieur," she said, her voice cold and grave from rigid self-control, "there is one thing of which I would speak to you, lest I might not have an opportunity when we reach Philadelphia. Monsieur," turning so she might face him, a slight tremor now perceptible in her tone, "I want you to know that I understood quite perfectly, quite perfectly what it must have meant to you to arrest Armand, and — and appreciate that it was the right thing for you to do. I never felt that he would be made to suffer the penalty of his crime, and perhaps that made a difference. But had my brother been punished, I think I should have tried even then to have understood how you were right in your way. And I think had they killed Armand, I should have been sorry for you too.   I should have been sorry for you too, Monsieur."

He saw her face lifted like a white flower in the dusk to his, and then he turned his glance away, greatly touched by her sweet words, but inexpressibly depressed as he felt that they betrayed no love, only the impulse of a just and generous nature.   And once he had thought to win her love!   He looked down at her again, at the clear eyes so full of child-like honesty and pleading, as if she craved his pardon for any injustice done him, while it was he who had brought suffering upon her, that he smiled grimly in the excess of emotion which surged up in his heart.   But the smile which had arisen from the tenderness she invariably aroused in him was colored by the infinite sadness of the hopelessness of that affection.

"Dear Mademoiselle," he said gently, "I should feel that you would always understand; that always you would be pitiful of the unfortunate.   And I doubt not that you would bestow your sympathy on me, too, for I am less happy than I seem.   Perhaps when you return to France you will think of me, sometimes, as a friend of yours, here in this distant land, and —and it would comfort me to think that you did."

"Yes," she repeated dully, "when I return to France — a friend in a distant land — I shall not forget, Monsieur."

The pause in which he had taken off his coat and his slow riding had left them a good distance behind the troops. Long since the Quakeress and her escort had disappeared from sight in the dusk, the soldier, much to the good dame's anxiety lest she should lose all track of her charge, insisting upon keeping up with his comrades, avowing it was discipline which demanded that he do so, although the simple soul behind him wondered if he did not also enjoy the conversation and joking of the men whose company he would not forego. The violet light of the evening had deepened into the purple night. The men stepped briskly, although the road was muddy and shadowed blackly by the forest on either side. But a full moon shone in a clear sky, and despite their physical weariness and the poor roads, they were singing, for hope springing lightly in the human breast finds only an incentive in opposition.

Chapter XV

WHERE the road diverged widely, a solitary apple tree stood in the centre of the highway. Here the moonlight streamed down broadly, lying whitely on the earth, silvering the dark green leaves of the tree and casting its shadow sharply down the road — an ominous and blighting shadow whispering of an evil reality. Since Mademoiselle de Berny passed beneath the spreading branches of this apple tree, the tight red buds had blown and fluttered in petals pink and white to the ground. Now the tree bore fruit prematurely — the bitter fruit of treason and revenge. Like an avenging arm one great branch stretched across the roadway. From it dangled a terrible burden, grayish in the moonlight, dragging down the heavy limb.

The troops grew silent; some of the men shuddered; others passed on hardened to such sights. One soldier, whose hatred burned as a fire which death might not quench, stooped and picked up a stone and flung it with a curse at the burden hanging from the tree, and then, still cursing, he walked on. Young Stirling was among the first to pass. He rode, mounted behind one of the soldiers, seated sideways as a woman. As it is whispered by old grand-dames that one has a prescience of death when that plot of earth which is to be his grave is trodden upon, so perhaps this boy, blind though he was, became aware of his proximity to that hanging figure, for he shivered and grew pale, as if he had drawn shudderingly back from the brink of a precipice over which he had nearly slipped, and fascinated by horror had watched a stone, dislodged by his foot, go whirling down the great abyss. He grew silent, singing no longer. The immense hound ran whining and snuffing around the tree seeking to attract his young master's attention, but the boy recalled him sharply and imperatively to his side, bidding him be still, after which he turned and put his arm around the stalwart figure of the soldier in front of him.

"Cannot your horse step more briskly, good friend?" he asked. "I think we are passing a long marsh, for this damp raw air chills me. And hear how my dog is complaining."

His companion glanced back pityingly over his shoulder at the boy, and then complying with his request touched the horse they rode lightly with the whip.

Reaching the place sometime later, Major Heyward's horse reared, snorting in affright. The young man spoke kindly to it, patting the animal's head and forcing it to proceed. But when they had passed the tree, he glancing

R

down at his companion saw that her eyes were staring and terror stricken, and that one of her hands clutched his sleeve fearfully.

"What was that?" she asked. So great was her terror that her voice sank to a whisper.

"Nothing, nothing but a shadow, Mademoiselle," he said, striving to speak lightly; "my horse is so restive that he jumps at the falling of a leaf."

But she, looking around, whispered again and again, and he saw that she was almost paralyzed with fear.

He took her hands in his, slipping the reins over his arm.

"Mademoiselle," he said gently, in the tone of voice one uses to a little child, "such things are not uncommon in war, and there must be examples made."

"Was it he?" she whispered, after a long silence.

He, divining that she meant the Quaker Roberts, answered in the affirmative.

She moved restlessly.

"And when the sun rises to-morrow he will still be there. Why did they leave him hanging so?"

"But yesterday was he hung, Mademoiselle," answered her companion. "He had been wounded when making his escape, and found refuge in a farm-house after wandering in the woods for nearly two days. See, Mademoiselle." He checked his horse momentarily to point out to her the low dark roof of a farm-house some distance away at the edge of the woods. "There he lay carefully nursed, and when he was quite recovered and about to make his way to Philadelphia, those who had nursed him betrayed him, in revenge for the wrongs he had perpetrated upon a son of their family who was a rebel prisoner in the city. It is a bitter tale, Mademoiselle, for so surely as a man soweth malice shall he reap malice, and those he treads under his foot shall turn even as the worm turns. The atrocious cruelties Roberts inflicted upon innocent country people and upon our prisoners are not to be lightly passed over. It is a righteous judgment that he should be left to hang, an example to traitors."

"But after he is dead," she whispered, "after he is dead! To hang like that without rest or peace. Could they not have cut him down and laid him on the ground? All my life I shall think of him like that, when the sky is blue, or when it is storming, he will still be hanging there. It is so cruel," she said piti-fully; "they did all they could to him. Why need they leave him there?"

Her voice was that of a person tormented beyond endurance, and she moved nervously.

"I shall never forget it," she said, "I shall never forget it." Her illness had left her highly strung and unable to bear patiently any shock.

The young man felt the cold trembling clasp of her hands upon his wrist. Her troubled voice went to his heart, and her weight as she leant against his arm was so light that the realization of that fact was inexpressibly painful to him. A great wave of passionate tenderness swept over him so that he was seized with a desire almost irresistible to clasp the fragile form to his breast, to hold her safe from death, from trouble, from all the world—to kiss the helpless and lovely face until the pale cheek brightened beneath his burning kiss. With a sigh he recalled his thought to the present and looked searchingly around him. From the road in front came the muffled sound of the steady tramping of the soldiers and the broken echo of their singing. The road was unsafe. A solitary traveller was exempt neither from marauding Tories nor Indians. As for the Quaker, he well deserved his fate. A woman's heart was tender and easily wounded, yet— He looked down at the little figure in his arms.

"Mademoiselle," he said, "would it make you happier were we to return and cut the body down?"

"Yes," she whispered.

He turned his horse and rode back. As they neared the place again his steed grew restive, so that he had great trouble in controlling it, but succeeded at last in quieting it and forcing it to stand still within a short distance of the tree. Then he dismounted.

"You will not fall, Mademoiselle?" he questioned anxiously. He drew his cloak more closely around her and gave her the reins to hold.

It was a strange and weird sight. The moonlight fell in white shaft-like lines on the broad expanse of road, making it seem smooth and bare. The sharply defined figures of the two young people and the horse were distinct as a silhouette. On either side of the highway rose the dark, almost impenetrable forest. There, a little off the road, within the shadows of its tall trees, the forest would guard the secret of a dishonored grave. Heyward fell directly to work. Now and then he glanced up at Mademoiselle's muffled little form on the horse, her trembling hand patting the animal's head to keep it quiet. Not a word was spoken. No sound was heard save the mournful cry of some night-bird, the dropping of a twig or leaf.

The young man worked rapidly. He had removed his hat, revealing his powdered hair, white as/ his ruffled shirt. The earth was soft and lightly packed. In a short time he had half dug a shallow grave by the aid of his broad sword and a tin plate from his knapsack. Looking up again at his companion to

assure himself of her safety, he observed two
Indian warriors, stragglers of the army, who
had paused on their way by and remained
motionless, spectators of the scene, strange
figures wrapped in blankets with feathered
head-gear and with dark aquiline profiles distinct in the soft brilliancy of the night.   Heyward bade them assist him, and the three
working together soon completed the task,
the Indians throwing up the earth with their
hands.   When the grave was finished Heyward and his two fellow-workers cut down
the huge and sad burden from the limb to
which it hung and which sprang up again
joyously.

"Put this over his face," said Mademoiselle
de Berny, and the young officer went and took
the handkerchief she extended.   But as he
knelt at the dead man's side a moment later,
and saw the face distorted by helpless rage and
agony of pain, the evil face to which death
brought no peace, he slipped the little handkerchief in his pocket, and drawing out his
own laid it instead over the lifeless face, and
then rising he and the Indians heaped the
earth quickly over the unshriven dead and
piled on leaves to quite conceal the grave.

At the completion of the task, Heyward
gave some coins to the Indians.   He picked
up his hat and drew his sword over the grass
to remove the earth clinging to it.   The tin

plate he flung away. As he turned around he saw that he and Mademoiselle de Berny were once more alone together. The two Indians had stolen mysteriously away. He ran his sword into its sheath and returned to Mademoiselle.

" It is done," he said briefly.

But she did not hear him. Her uplifted face, spirit-like in the moonlight, her lips moving, her hands holding her rosary, proved to him that she was praying. Silently he bowed his head and waited until she had finished, then mounted behind her, and turning his horse once more rode rapidly.

Suddenly her head sank wearily against him. But at the touch the bitterness in his heart sprang into new life. For one moment thus, then she would leave him forever. In little less than an hour they would be in Philadelphia.

" Mademoiselle de Berny," he said, " I must ask your pardon for the position in which I have placed you. But at the time and also now it seemed the only thing I could do under the circumstances. You were so unprotected, that I allowed the good woman ahead of us to believe me your betrothed husband lest some rough soldier should be made your escort, as the other officers beside myself whom you knew in camp are with His Excellency. But in a little while you will be rid of me, and I shall never trouble you further."

Bitterly he awaited her reply, but she did not speak.

Suddenly there broke forth a sob, followed by others, heart-breaking and uncontrollable.

For one second it seemed to him as if the agony in his own heart had found voice.

There was a pause, then the pitiful sobs broke forth again. He caught her to his breast, understanding at last. His voice broke with pain and longing.

" Diane," he said, " oh, Diane ! "

In the desperate need of each for the other's sympathy after the trials they had passed through, they remained silent in a close embrace — a silence stirred only by Mademoiselle's low sobbing. Her cheek was pressed to his, her tears were on his lips. In his arms she was trembling as a bird which had flown far and found rest. And at last she grew quiet and soothed; her grief had sobbed itself out upon his breast, and her tears had ceased to flow. He drew her arm around his neck. On his he felt the touch of her sweet mouth and the words between them remaining unspoken were yet understood. And so through the moonlit night they rode, — her head upon his shoulder and his arm around her, — two young lovers in the midst of war, yet for whom life just then held naught but peace. The vague perfumes, the murmurings and the soft breezes of the spring night, surrounded them, and above their heads were the unclouded heavens.

And after a while words came, whispered words upon his shoulder, until at last her eyes met his, shyly, but revealing a love unspeakable. He looked down at her lying against his breast, blushing with love in the moonshine, smiling as one whose supreme desire is fulfilled. She stirred a little in his arms.

"Where is Armand?" she said, and raised herself to search the road in front of them with anxious gaze.

"The troops are well in advance," he answered; "but he is safe with them, and I, myself, put him in charge of a worthy fellow."

But he could not quiet her suddenly awakened anxiety.

"There is no one," she said, "no one who is always in my heart as he is."

"And I, sweetheart," he asked smiling, "what of me?"

"You," she said, "ah, Richard, that is different, you are mine, you belong to me, as I to you. But since his father died, he has been alone in the world. Once I thought that I could be all to him, but that was before I came to Valley Forge. Now," she added sadly, "I know it will never be so, for I have learned to know him better, and he is lonely for his father. Ah, Richard, Richard, death could not separate us!"

He spoke assuring words to her, until once more she smiled entirely comforted.

"Richard," she said at last, with grave reproach, "there is one thing I shall not forgive you — that you destroyed the only love-letter you ever wrote me. A woman would not have been so stupid!"

They had reached a long low hill-line, from the ridge of which could be seen the lights of Philadelphia. On the moonlit road below, between them and the city, they could see the black moving mass of the Continental troops.

Heyward checked the horse for a moment. Mademoiselle de Berny leant forward, her gaze sweeping the landscape.

"What a great country is this, Richard," she said. "See how the city lies like a little cluster of village lights nestling near the river. How the land stretches away on all sides of us, seeming vast and limitless as the sky above us, did we not know that beyond lay the ocean."

"And will you be content to stay here, Diane?" he asked. "We have none such great cities as you are accustomed to in the Old World, but on the other hand we hear not the wailing of the poor which rises from the streets of those cities. We have no brilliant court society, yet neither do we hear the murmurings of an oppressed people who are powerless to throw off the chains which hold them slaves to the will of a despot. And when this war is

over, Diane, and victory is ours, then you and
I will take long journeys together, and you will
learn the grandeur of this new republic, with
its great mountains and rivers; a land which is
divided into no petty kingdoms, and whose
limitations are marked only by the hand of
God in His great oceans on either side."

Mademoiselle de Berny smiled a little wist-
fully. She rested her head against him once
more, and her hand slipped into his.

"Richard," she said, "the greatness of your
country frightens me, — I who have stepped
but little beyond the convent walls and the gay
society of the French court. You must not
reproach me if sometimes in the future I have
a homesickness for my sunny France; for
the love of it runs in my blood. Yet I shall
have no regret at remaining here with you; for
has it not always been so — that the woman
gives up her country to make her home where
the man she loves makes his?"

"Sweetheart," he said, "love knows no
country."

She laughed. "Yet, Richard," she murmured mischievously, "you would not go
back with me and live in France."

"My country needs me here, Diane," he
answered gravely.

"If it needs you, then it needs me also," she
said; "for love makes us one, Richard."

"Diane," he said, holding her closer in his

arms, "we can find the lilies that you love
here.   We call them not the Fleur-de-lis as
you do in France, nor do we give them the
old English name of Flower-de-luce; but in
this country we call them the Sweet Flag, and
I will take you to the great marshes where you
may see them blowing white and purple, mile
on mile."

"Yes," she whispered, "we will go there together, you and I, when the war is over.   And
Armand, Richard?   He, too, will gather the
lilies with us."

He laughed.

"When the war is over," he repeated happily,
and kissed her.   This night seemed the reason
why he had lived, for him, he thought; whatever the future held, it was worthy that his
future life should exist that he might remember
it.   He bent his head to lay his face against
hers.

"Ah, dear   Mademoiselle," he whispered
chokingly; "ah, dear Mademoiselle!"

Chapter XVI

IN the fall of that year, on a golden morning in late October, there rode out from the city of New York three persons, one of the riders being accompanied by a hound. Two of these people were Mademoiselle de Berny and her brother, and the third member of the party was a priest mounted on a white mule. The journey had interfered with the latter's routine service, and he strove to soothe his conscience by chanting the service of the hour in Latin.

The sun, bright in a clear sky, shone warmly on their backs and cast their shadows ahead of them down the forest road. The purple haze of Indian summer filled the air, which had the balminess of spring. Here the breeze had swept the road bare, but there the horses stepped knee deep in drifts of rustling leaves. Some few yellow leaves still hung trembling on the naked branches. Now and again there flamed a late scarlet maple.

One month ago Mademoiselle de Berny had received a letter from her uncle, the Abbé de Berny, in which he stated his wish to have her return to France that fall. When the message reached her she was in New York, where the

British held possession of the city. General
Stirling had, within a few days after her return
to Philadelphia from Valley Forge, sent for
her and his nephew, and placed them in the
care of Tory friends in New York. With the
exception of those few days in Philadelphia, she
and Richard Heyward had not seen each other,
although the two had been able to maintain
a desultory correspondence by means of an
Indian. Since receiving word from her uncle,
Mademoiselle de Berny had written in greatest
anxiety to her lover, desiring that she might
return to France as his wife, thus protected from
all plans her uncle doubtless intended regarding
her marriage. The letter sent by the Indian
was received and immediately answered by
Heyward.

The first lull in the activities of war was
seized by the lovers, and the time and place of
the marriage settled upon. General Stirling
was away on a campaign, and his absence fur-
thered the plan ; while the Tories, in whose care
Mademoiselle had been placed, were a gay and
pleasure-loving company who allowed her great
freedom. Heyward, obtaining a furlough for
two days, journeyed on horseback to an inn some
eight miles distant from New York. Nearer
the enemy's lines at that particular time it was
not expedient to approach. He reached the
tavern the night preceding his wedding day,
and found the Indian awaiting him there, — a

courier sent in advance by Mademoiselle de
Berny to inform him that she would arrive in
the middle of the following morning.

He was awake early the next morning, awaiting impatiently the coming of his bride. Two
ancient roads, now seldom used, led from New
York to the inn, and not knowing which one
would be taken by Mademoiselle de Berny he
did not ride forward to meet her, but remained
at the tavern, strolling a little way down one
road and back again and then down the other.

And not far distant Mademoiselle de Berny
also waxed impatient of the intervening miles.

" Oh, do let us hasten, Armand ! " she said,
"the road runs straight." She touched her horse
with her whip and young Stirling followed suit.

Another moment and their horses were
flying side by side; the fresh air blowing in
their faces; the road and the priest vanishing
behind them. At last they turned, exhilarated
by the brisk canter, and rode slowly back to
meet their companion, whose mule ambled
contentedly along and was not to be hurried.

" Armand," said Mademoiselle de Berny,
" you are to give away the bride."

" Thus would my father have done had he
lived," he answered. " Bethink yourself, Diane,
'tis not yet too late to withdraw. Do you not
know it would grieve my father that you should
marry a rebel, rather than a loyal subject of the
King or a man of our mother's nationality ? "

"Oh, love, love!" laughed Mademoiselle de Berny, turning her horse around by the side of the priest as the two reached him, "it is more than religion, is it not, Father Da Gamo, inasmuch as it knows neither party nor country? See," dropping the reins of her horse and extending both her pretty hands, "held I one hour of love in this palm and all eternity in that, pouf — so, even so could I blow eternity away, of such light weight would it be compared to that one hour. Ah, Father, e'en beneath your cassock does not your heart acknowledge 'tis a right good thing to love?"

"Fain art thou to speak lightly of things holy, my child," answered the little priest; "sorely against my will didst thou persuade me to come with thee to-day; notwithstanding our most reverend Father hath sanctioned this alliance with a Protestant. But women prevail upon us by their sweet voices. Yet if marriage thou wilt have, better one sanctified by love, although thou art disobedient unto those in authority and breakest a lesser commandment."

"But you do not answer my question," she pursued. "Now tell me did you never love? Does your cassock not hide a wounded heart, Father?"

The little priest crossed himself.

"Heaven hath been merciful unto me. Fain would I repeat to you the words of St. Paul, who desired that all men were even as himself, saying that every man hath his 'proper gift of God, one after this manner and another after that, — he that is unmarried careth for things that belongeth to the Lord; but he that is married careth for the things that are of the world, how he may please his wife."

"Oh, why will you be so doleful on my marriage morning?" she cried. "Think you of naught which is cheerful to say?"

She glanced from the priest to her brother and back again impatiently.

"If you were going to my funeral, and you should show e'en there not less sorry countenances, my ghost should play a few pranks to make you merry. Armand, dear heart, you oppress me so that my eyes are full of tears. You would not have a bride weep on her wedding morn?"

He smiled brightly.

"I would have you never weep, Diane. Guide my horse," he added, handing her the reins, "and I will play for you."

Through the forest glades rang the music of his flute, soaring lightly as a bird's song, falling deeply, mournfully as human woe. But after a little he changed the tune and a more joyous melody filled the air.

Thus did Mademoiselle de Berny hear her wedding march.

On her brother's saddle was fastened the bridal bouquet which he had gathered in the gar-

s

den of their New York residence and arranged
with infinite care.   He was dressed as a wedding
guest, perfumed and bejewelled.   For the first
time since his father's death had he consented
to remove his mourning attire.   This change in
his attire he had himself suggested.

" For I would also be gayly decked on thy
bridal morn, Diane, lest my sober garb should
sadden you," he had said with deep gravity.
Now he wore a coat of dark gray satin with
high collar and broad lapels ; at his breast and
wrists were full ruffles ; his double-breasted
waistcoat was of white silk embroidered in pink
rosebuds ; his knee breeches and silken hose
were of a lighter shade of gray than his coat.
His fair hair was powdered and worn in a queue,
tied with a black velvet ribbon.   He wore a
boutonnière of rosebuds with their green leaves.
On the collar of the Great Dane he had fastened
a similar cluster of flowers, with loving insistence
that the hound was also a wedding guest.   Since
his experience at Valley Forge a subtle change
had made itself felt in young Stirling.   He had
matured, growing graver and more composed
than hitherto.   His face seemed to have become
longer and more delicate, and so great was the
contrast now between the waxen immobility of
his countenance and the rich and glowing ani-
mation of Mademoiselle's face, that the great
family resemblance between them was barely
noticeable.

Of Mademoiselle de Berny's dress naught could be seen. Her plumed hat shadowed her face. Her crimson cardinal, lined with fur, was clasped together. But now and then beneath the fur edge a slender foot revealed itself, clad in a white satin shoe with a broad buckle a-twinkle in the sunshine.

The wild sweet music of the flute was the first intimation of her approach to her lover.

As the little party neared the tavern, and Mademoiselle de Berny beheld the tall figure of the young officer in full-dress uniform of blue and buff, his head bared and turned impatiently in her direction, a great shyness seized upon her so that she could not meet his glance. He, lifting her from her horse, saw the little shoe, and, divining the hidden bridal gown, held her closely, as if he would never release her; and her face upon his shoulder was the color of a rose.

The marriage service was very simple. It took place in the principal room of the tavern, with the aged host and his wife and their maid-servant as witnesses. The two women had made such decoration as they might upon so short a notice and with only the most primitive means at their command. The floor was white and sanded and the corners decorated with branches of fir and scarlet maple, while pale forest flowers and ferns and the purple sumach were arranged in pitchers and bowls.

At one side of the room was a table loaded with viands and fruit. After the ceremony this table was drawn out to the centre of the room. And the bride would have mine host and his wife seated at the table, and the maid-servant only to wait upon the company. Even the Indian guide she insisted should be seated. The little priest waxed jovial, pledging the health of all present in the mellow wine, speaking thickly at last so that the bride's eyes danced with merriment. The Indian alone seemed unmoved, his inscrutable dark face expressionless, his eyes fastened on his plate. Amidst the jest and merriment, young Stirling startled them by affirming that he heard a distant tramping of horses. The hound, crouched at his master's feet, raised his head growling. After a moment's anxious silence, which revealed no sound, the merriment waxed louder, the hound being sharply ordered to be silent. To this little and obscure tavern at the crossing of two roads seldom used, a belated traveller sometimes made his way. Otherwise the guests were few.

The eyes of the newly made wife grew wistful. Already the shadow of parting was upon her. Across the table her eyes met those of her young husband.

"See, sweetheart," he said, "I bring you a philopena." In his hand he held a nut with twin kernels. As he rose and went towards her, he passed the open casement and saw several mounted Tories as they swung around a curve of the road some rods away.

In an all embracing glance around the room, he saw no chance of concealment in the primitive building. His glance fell last upon the Indian who had half risen from the table. His attitude had the alert pose of a wild thing about to spring. The plot was revealed to Heyward in a flash. The Indian had sold him to the Tories. His face white with passion, the young man made one stride towards the fellow and seized him by the back of the neck.

" You dog ! " he cried, " you miserable cur ! " shaking the writhing creature in his powerful grasp. With contempt too deep for vengeance he flung him into a corner of the room.

" Watch him ! " he commanded the hound. In another second he had run the bar of the door to and was pushing the table in front of it to gain time. He looked at his companions stricken with terror and staring questioningly at him ; the sudden pallor on the priest's face ; the blind boy talking wildly, his face tragic in its baffled eagerness. At one side of the room the miserable maid-servant, who had caught a glimpse of the Tories, crouched screaming, with her hands over her ears. In the further corner the hound, growling, with his teeth fastened in the dark throat of the Indian, was worrying his victim to death. The situation was hopeless.

There was no one to whom he could look for help.

There was heard the sound of the new arrivals as they drew up their horses and dismounted. But there was none to receive them nor bid them welcome. The barred door met them inhospitably and inimically. Behind it shivered the old innkeeper and his wife.

Heavy steps ascended the verandah, followed by a loud knocking with the handle of a whip upon the door.

Heyward glanced at his bride and put her behind him.

"Diane," he said, "for God's sake stay behind me."

He drew his sword and listened intently at the door. Suddenly he turned and caught his wife in his arms and kissed her.

"God forgive me, Diane," he said hoarsely, "for having brought this upon you."

There was repeated the knocking, followed by a violent kicking. Were it this door alone to guard, no entrance could be made save over his dead body. He realized afresh the hopelessness of his position with the casements unguarded as well as the back entrance. Like infuriated beasts would these Tories, clamoring for admittance, burst into the room upon the unprotected women, the helpless boy and priest —better to meet them outside, to run the risk of being made a prisoner and chance his escape.

But he would sell his freedom as dearly as possible. As he was about to draw the bolt, he found at his side an unexpected ally. The little priest stood resolutely near him, his fat face white and flabby from fear, but a dauntless light in his eyes.

"I will go first," he said. "Stand away," he called loudly, "and I will open the door unto you."

There was a muttered curse and a gruff assent.

Father Da Gamo opened the door and stepped outside, his round black figure with outstretched arms barring the way.

There were four men crowded on the little verandah. Their ruffianly and swaggering air, their faces red and bloated from carousals, proved them to be of the worst class of Tories, — native Americans whose outrages and atrocities made them more bitterly feared and hated than the Indians. They were licensed outlaws, armed and uniformed at the expense of the King, but dependent upon their own resources for provision and money. They were not only permitted but encouraged to enrich themselves by the plunder of the rebels. They were far more mischievous and malignant enemies of their country than its foreign invaders.

The foremost of the men who had ascended the verandah fell back, hesitating to lay sacrilegious hands on a priest. But catching a glimpse of the buff and blue uniform of the officer a second later, he flung the priest aside with an oath. Ere he obtained entrance Heyward sprang at him with upraised chair, bringing the implement crashing down on the fellow's head and shoulders, so that he reeled and tumbled back among his comrades, who also fell back, but rallied and made a heavy onslaught at the doorway. The body of their injured leader writhing at their feet was pushed half over the threshold, one of the men stumbling over him, but regaining his balance before he fell.

Heyward, fighting desperately with his sword, managed to make his way out upon the verandah, from whence he was driven backwards down the steps. He retreated to a tree whose huge trunk protected his back, while he strove to keep the enemy at bay. With two only against whom to contend he might have won, but the odds were against him with three. It was now but a question of moments before he would be made a prisoner.

Suddenly the little priest, bending over the Tory who lay groaning loudly on the threshold, straightened himself and pointed toward a gap in the forest.

"A-a-ah!" he cried loudly and triumphantly, still pointing, "thou hast lost the rarest bird, my friends!"

The ruse succeeded.

One of the Tories turned, cursing, dropping his sword to his side. "Keep an eye on the dog," he nodded to the other two. He strode toward the tavern muttering, hurling maledictions at the priest whom he believed to have assisted another if not more of the Continental rebels to escape.

The priest had dragged the wounded Tory into the room and was succoring the man as best he could. At the entrance there appeared suddenly the slender figure of young Stirling. The ruffian made an unsuccessful pass at him with his sword, tearing his satin coat, but not grazing his flesh. Before Mademoiselle de Berny could follow her impulse to thrust herself between her brother and his assailant, the boy had put her aside, and raising his sword bore down upon his opponent.

The next few moments witnessed a strange and unprecedented encounter. For the boy drove the Tory into a corner of the verandah. No movement of his foe escaped him. He parried every thrust, locating the man with unfaltering accuracy. To this mysterious encounter, between the seeing and the blind, there was but one witness. Heyward, his entire energy bent upon escaping from the two men who only guarded him now, saw nothing of the scene upon the verandah, which was screened by vines. The priest in the interior of the tavern still ministered to the wounded Tory. But

Mademoiselle de Berny in her white bridal gown, her hands pressed to her breast, leant against the wall paralyzed by fear, unable to speak or move. The green wavering shadows of the vine fell on the two. Once young Stirling pushed back the lace ruffle hanging over his hand. It seemed as if some superhuman power were invested in him and he were playing with his enemy, so light and graceful was his erect and slender form in the wedding garb of pink and gray. The silence which up to this time had barely been disturbed by the light movements of the two opponents was now broken by the stentorian breathing of the Tory growing louder and more labored, until it was like the panting of an animal. His full face grew purple, his hair was matted to his forehead with perspiration. Desperately he made a lunge at his opponent which, had it proven successful, would have ended the duel. But his hand faltered and his glance swerved as the Great Dane, growling, emerged from the doorway. Another second and the animal sprang past his master at the Tory's throat. With scarcely an effort the man flung the hound off and leaped over the railing of the verandah, running terror-stricken towards his horse. The blood was flowing from a wound in his left arm made by young Stirling's blade.

The Great Dane, still growling ominously,

lay huddled in a heap on the floor of the verandah. The reason of his inability to hold the
Tory, and the ease with which the man had flung
him off, was made apparent by a wound in his
side from the knife of the Indian he had been
guarding.

Young Stirling's voice rose shrilly, crying
triumphantly after his foe: " Run, run, coward! Coward!"

Of the two Tories guarding Heyward, one
turned. The occupants of the verandah were
screened by the close green vine; but hearing
the moaning of the hound he mistook the
sound for the groans of his comrade whom he
had seen go up the steps of the porch, and
whom he still supposed to be there, not having
witnessed his escape. He ran toward the inn,
shouting his coming to the companion he in-
ferred was there and in need of his assistance.

Heyward, horrified by those sounds which
revealed to him that either his bride or her
brother were in danger, made a desperate effort,
and thrust aside the one man left guarding him.

Young Stirling, hearing the approach of the
Tory, turned toward the steps of the verandah.
As he passed his sister he put out his left arm
and drew her toward him. As the man came
up the steps,— Heyward following closely,—
the boy bore down upon him, descending as
the fellow retreated. And he had but one
arm free, for the other encircled his sister. He

raised his sword and brought it swinging down. It grazed the fellow's shoulder. With an oath the man turned, eluded Heyward, and fled to his horse, and mounting rode away as one pursued by devils, and perceiving for the first time the comrade whom he would have assisted galloping madly down the road a good distance ahead of him. The last Tory, who had once more assailed Heyward, had his sword struck from his hand and fled also for dear life.

Young Stirling stepped down upon the ground and advanced a little way. Then, his progress deterred by the weight of his sister whom he still held, and who had lost consciousness, he stood still, listening. Upon his shoulder drooped her head with closed eyes. Their natural relation seemed inverted. He now protected her. As he heard the galloping of the Tories' horses, and the groans of the dying man from the interior of the inn, he laughed softly.

"Diane, you will not again say—"

He paused suddenly, and the smile on his face died. The lace ruffles above his heart were moved by the violent throbbing. He raised his sword, shining wet and scarlet, straight above his head, his face lifted in the dazzling sunlight.

"My father," he cried in a loud voice of piercing sweetness, "my father, thou beholdest me!"

A moment longer he stood erect, then droping his sword, fell backward. Heyward caught his wife away just in time to save her from falling also.

The little priest had come out upon the verandah.

"Merciful God," he mumbled in a weak voice like a woman's. "Merciful God, with mine eyes have I beheld a miracle. Thou hast given sight unto the blind!"

Heyward was holding the senseless form of his bride, murmuring mad and incoherent words in his frenzy of grief lest she were dead.

Young Stirling lay stretched upon the ground as one forgotten. Yet not quite alone, for the Great Dane, hearing that last exultant cry, came from the tavern but barely able to drag itself along. The blood was flowing from the wound made by the Indian's knife. The hound came lurching heavily down the steps, and had dragged itself almost to its master's feet when it fell down. But still it managed to work its way, bleeding along the dusty road, until with a dying effort it licked the lifeless hand.

Chapter XVII

MADEMOISELLE de Berny's bridal dress was stained by blood flowing from a wound in her shoulder, which she had received during her brother's brief encounter with the last Tory he had driven away.

But Armand was unscathed. He lay as he had fallen, the arm which had encircled her still retaining the curve of that last embrace; his other arm and hand outstretched stiffly held his sword. He was smiling strangely, but the wonderful light which the priest had beheld in his sightless eyes was quenched in death.

With Mademoiselle remained the grief of the living.

The news of her marriage came as a great blow to her uncle, the Abbé de Berny. This last flower of his family, possessing his entire love, had wedded an obscure soldier in an almost unknown country. For her had he arranged a brilliant alliance, and the proposed husband was to take the bride's name and thus perpetuate the honored and dying family of de Berny.

But within a few years the bitter regret softened into resignation and later became

thankfulness that she was spared the horrors
of the French Revolution. The man to whom
he would have married her died on the guillo-
tine.   He saw his high estate and his vast
fortune swept from him.   Waiting in his prison
for the blessed relief of death, longing for peace,
he thought of her as of one in a now serene
and untroubled country, and thanked God that
she was happy.

General Stirling returned to England after
the war, but within a year came back to
America.

"Diane," he said huskily, "I am an old
man. Let me have my home with you."

And Diane.   She saw peace and honor come
to her adopted country, beheld her husband
governor of his state.

In the spring and fall of every year Governor
and Lady Heyward made a journey north to a
grave lying near a deserted tavern in a forest.
And sometimes it seemed to Diane that the
sweetest love she ever gave, that which was
maternal in her nature, lay buried there. For
she had no children. All the infinite and tender
yearning of an unfulfilled motherhood centred
in that little grave, whereon the grass grew soft
and green between her and Armand.

And amidst the petty realities and the heavy
responsibilities that life brings, the thought of
that dim forest was ever with her. Her heart
was divided between the living and the dead.

In her thought the silent wild woods where her brother slept became a garden to her — a garden of Paradise where her dead would come back to her, and once more she would kiss those lips so many days unkissed. Again she would feel him so long bereft of her embrace, resting at last within her arms now aching with loneliness ; and again she would hear the exultant boyish voice.

THE END